(28)

THE
YOUNG
NURSES

THE
YOUNG
NURSES

Jane Converse

G.K. Hall & Co. • Chivers Press
Thorndike, Maine USA   Bath, England

This Large Print edition is published by G.K. Hall & Co., USA
and by Chivers Press, England.

Published in 2000 in the U.S. by arrangement with Maureen Moran.

Published in 2001 in the U.K. by arrangement with the author.

U.S. Softcover   0-7838-9281-0 (Paperback Series Edition)
U.K. Hardcover 0-7540-4378-9 (Chivers Large Print)

The text of this Large Print edition is unabridged.
Other aspects of the book may vary from the original edition.

Set in 16 pt. Plantin by Anne Bradeen.

Printed in the United States on permanent paper.

British Library Cataloguing-in-Publication Data available

Library of Congress Cataloging-in-Publication Data

Converse, Jane.
    The young nurses / by Jane Converse.
      p. cm.
    ISBN 0-7838-9281-0 (lg. print : sc : alk. paper)
    1. Nurses — Fiction. 2. Large type books.   I. Title.
PS3553.O544 Y68 2000
 813'.54—dc21   00-061469

THE
YOUNG
NURSES

ONE

"If you want to keep friends," Aunt Cammie said, probably for the thousandth time that Janet Leland could remember, "keep your advice to yourself."

Janet sank down in the sofa that dominated the homey living room, taking her place beside Lloyd Turner. Outside, the red brick streets still reflected the heat of the August afternoon, though they had finished dinner an hour ago. ("Danforth, Ohio, heat," Aunt Cammie called it, as though this state, and this old university town in particular, possessed its own private weather.) "That helps a lot, darling," Janet said. "I ask you an important question and you give me your old bromide about not giving advice. Thanks heaps."

Cammie's wide, round face stretched in a quick grimace. This was as close to smiling as Janet's aunt ever came. In the next instant she assumed her more typically dour expression. "Have I ever told you what to do, Janet? Have I *ever?* No. People learn by doing, not by being told. When your mother passed away and my brother asked me to move in here and take charge, I made up my mind I wasn't going to go down in history as a . . . dictatorial spinster. A spinster, yes. A bossy one, no. I said, 'Frank, I love that little girl and I'll see to it that she doesn't lack for a thing. But I'm going to live *my* life, and I'm going to let Janet live *hers,* and we're going to remain friends.'" Aunt Cammie stopped to peer critically at the elephant she was carving out of a bar of Ivory soap, flicking a few white shavings from her navy polka-dotted dress to the newspaper she had spread out on the floor at her feet. She blinked her small, birdlike eyes with smug satisfaction. "Personally, I think my philosophy's worked out rather well."

Janet laughed, winking at the man who sat beside her. "Would you agree, Lloyd? D'you think Aunt Cammie's done a good job of raising me?"

Lloyd Turner grinned. Like everyone else who knew Aunt Cammie, he respected her, but didn't take the eccentric, fiftyish woman's unbending pronouncements seriously. "Oh, I don't know. She didn't teach you anything about being cautious in money matters. By the way, how old was Janet when you applied this do-it-yourself theory, Cammie?"

"Four and a half." Janet answered for her aunt. "And, you know, honey, it's *true!* She'll do anything in the world for me, but just try to get her opinion on anything! Before my dad died, four years ago, I could get advice from him. Should I go into nurses' training? Should we keep this big old house, when three of the bedrooms haven't been used in years? *Any* question, and Dad would at least give an *opinion*. Aunt Cammie. . . ."

"My brother, rest his soul, knew absolutely nothing about how to get along with people," Cammie announced in a prim tone. She patted her coarse, short-clipped salt-and-pepper hair with a soap-flecked hand. "Look, Janet. If you want to rent out two of the upstairs bedrooms, it's your house and you're perfectly free to do so. Not that it's any of my business, but. . . ."

"But it *is* your business!" Janet exclaimed. "You do all the cooking and cleaning. I'm at the hospital all day. . . ."

"And you're out with Lloyd half the rest of the time," Cammie finished brusquely. "Very well. I run the house for you, and, in exchange, I have a home here. That doesn't give me the right to tell you that you shouldn't take in roomers. If you can get approval from the hospital, or whoever decides whether a place is suitable for student nurses, go right ahead." Cammie appraised the whittled trunk of her fake ivory elephant. "If *I* were doing it, I'd offer room *and* board. I cook for the two of us anyway. Two more won't matter, and there's more money in it. I *presume* you're contemplating the idea for financial reasons? There's no. . . ."

"She's doing it because she loaned me every dime her father left her," Lloyd cut in. "All ten thousand dollars of it."

"Will you stop it?" Janet demanded. "That was a . . . well, not a *loan*. If a girl can't let her future husband use the silly money to start his practice, then they shouldn't be thinking of getting married at all."

Janet turned to catch the faintly embittered expression on Lloyd's handsome face. How senseless it was for him to cling to that touchy pride of his! Lloyd had offered to share the rest of his life with her, hadn't he? And he had needed that ten thousand dollars to equip his office, hadn't he? Not that he couldn't have acquired everything he needed on credit, but what had been wrong with talking Lloyd into an arrangement that would save hundreds of dollars in interest? It was going to be *their* money when they became man and wife only a few months from now.

Janet's thoughts drifted momentarily from the practical issue under discussion to the planned Christmastime wedding. Lloyd had chosen the date; he would be celebrating the first anniversary of his acceptance by the Danforth Hospital Board late in December. If only he didn't talk about having the money repaid by then! As though it mattered, when two people loved each other. . . .

"I don't want to talk about money," Janet said. She let a few seconds pass, firmly establishing that the subject was closed, before she launched another. "The Supervisor of Nursing Services told me last week she's desperate for housing this year — for the September crop of student nurses. And when I told her I lived in this enormous old house, with a big old-fashioned porch and. . . ."

"And a squirrely aunt who carves soap statues," Cammie interrupted. "And raises meat-eating plants in a hothouse and can tell you the batting average of every player in the National League since 1931. I'm sure the lady said that the house sounds fine, but she has reservations about exposing impressionable young students to your crazy relatives." Aunt Cammie stomped to her feet and pounded across the living room toward the staircase, carrying her soap elephant and the newspaper full of shavings. "Use your own judgment, Janet. Goodnight, Dr. Turner. My fabulous apple pie for dessert tomorrow night. Be here if you aren't busy with some grisly job."

Lloyd suppressed a laugh; Aunt Cammie's bluntness was a guaranteed chink in the armor of his seriousness. "I'll try to cancel all my grisly jobs tomorrow," he assured her.

Cammie was out of sight by now, but apparently she had hesitated at the foot of the stairway. "Dr. Turner?"

"Yes?"

"You won't forget about bringing the tongue depressors?"

"I won't forget."

Janet waited until her aunt had clomped up the stairs. *"Tongue depressors?"*

Lloyd's arm fell around her shoulders. "She found a plan for a wren house in some old magazine. Supposed to be made out of Popsicle sticks, but she thought of all those neat, wide wooden depressors in my office. It makes sense. If I had my heart set on building a wren house, I'd see a doctor myself."

Janet shook her head. "What a character!"

"There should be millions more," Lloyd said, meaning it.

"I know." Janet paused while Lloyd planted a series of kisses on her temple. "What do you think, darling? Am I asking too much of Cammie? I mean, inviting two perfect strangers into the house — there'll be extra work. I figured she could earn a few dollars for all her hobbies. And her World Series fund — she's been talking about seeing the series next year."

"Sure."

"And it would be such a great help to whoever moves in. A home atmosphere. I know how lucky I was, being able to live right here while I trained. I talk to nurses at the hospital who lived in little dormitory rooms for three years and, at least during the first few months, felt awfully home-sick. I could give the girls some help with their homework while I'm here. . . ."

"While you're *here?*"

Janet felt her face coloring. "Lloyd, I'm not going to expect you to move into the same house with my aunt. And it'd break her heart to have to move out of this old place. When we're married, we'll want a little place of our own. Meanwhile, Cammie will have an income from boarders, and she won't feel like somebody's poor relative."

Lloyd's grip tightened around her shoulders. "Always planning the best of all possible worlds for everybody. If you ask me, Jan, I think you're asking for headaches. But I love you for your good intentions. Matter of fact, if the college doesn't find housing for more student nurses this fall, they may end up with half-filled classrooms. I have a vested interest in seeing those classrooms filled."

"You won't mind, then. . . ."

Lloyd hugged her. "Honey, I'm your future husband, I'm not a dictator. It's your house."

At times it was a little hard to believe. Dad, who had been almost as eccentric as his sister, had left only a token sum to Cammie in his will. The two-storied white-and-gray frame house, with its old-fashioned balustrades and its wide-screened porch had been deeded to Janet, with the provision that Aunt Cammie would be allowed to stay as long as she chose to.

Still, in spite of legal papers that said otherwise, the house was really Cammie's. She had decorated it with the results of her innumerable hobbies: glassed-in shelves of rose-decorated plates that dated back to her china painting phase; assorted throw rugs that had been woven, braided or hooked — depending on which craft was being taught at the time in the Danforth Adult Evening School; the portable hothouse outside the dining room, in which Cammie raised Venus's fly-traps and other plants listed under the "exotic" category in nursery catalogues.

There were touches of Aunt Cammie everywhere, though the original furniture, bought by Janet's mother, remained unchanged. There was a general outdated look to the overstuffed pieces, and a few times in recent years Janet had thought about replacing the kitchen linoleum or modernizing the upstairs and downstairs bathrooms, but any new item would have rendered the rest of the furnishings shabby by contrast. Janet had her job and her future to think about, and the house was her aunt's province; a complete remodelling job, or fresh decor, would have broken sentimental ties with the past. Besides, the money Janet had inherited was more wisely invested in her future with the young doctor. And the cash from renting the extra rooms. . . .

Janet shook herself out of this vague introspection. "I'm glad you approve," she said. Lloyd kissed her, and she closed her eyes, visualizing his perfectly defined yet ruggedly masculine features, the wavy black hair that often grew too long and curled at the nape of his neck — because he was "too busy to waste time in a barber's chair," the usually serious deep-blue eyes that lighted up when Janet said something foolishly feminine or when Cammie made one of her unsubtle statements. Janet twined her arms around Lloyd's neck and thought of how fortunate she was to have his love, to have Cammie's unflowery yet sincere devotion, to have a rewarding, fullfiling job, and to know that she was more than just passably attractive — because

Lloyd had not been the first man to compliment her on wide dark eyes that had been blessed with long upturned lashes, her chestnut colored hair that fell into soft waves with no more than a flick of a comb, and her figure — one that had made life among interns a sometimes embarrassing series of wolf whistles. Even the freckles sprinkled over her faintly upturned nose were an asset now (she had hated them as a child): Lloyd said they gave her a "gamin look."

So much to be thankful for! And . . . yes, she was even grateful for this marvelous old barn of a house!

She could not share her other good fortune with the two student nurses who would be moving in next week, but the easygoing home atmosphere that pervaded these rooms could be shared. In Lloyd's embrace she felt such profound happiness that she wished it were possible to parcel it out and distribute a portion to everyone else in the world. It was impossible, of course. But, making life brighter for two youngsters who had chosen her own profession — wasn't that the least she could do?

TWO

If someone had planned a drastic contrast between the two student nurses who moved into
the Leland home early in September, the result
could not have been more successful.

Beth de Haven was the first to arrive, and her
arrival was almost as spectacular as her appearance. Aunt Cammie, who was waiting on the
screened porch with Janet, drew an amazed
breath as the yellow Jaguar that had just torn
past the house came to a screeching halt, then
roared in reverse down the usually quiet, elm-
lined street. The tires of the flashy car squeaked
against the brick curbings, as its driver looked
over her shoulder to peer at the house number.
In the next instant, as Cammie and Janet recov-
ered from their shock over the erratic driving and
started for the screen door, a lithe blond creature
leaped out of the sports car and hurried, with
what might have been airy dance steps, up the
marigold-bordered walk.

Janet's first impression was one of incredibly
fresh, almost childlike loveliness. The girl had
long, straight, golden-yellow hair held with a
pale blue headband that gave her a resemblance to
illustrations for Alice in Wonderland. The little-
girl look was not dispelled by a closer look at her

face as she approached. She had soft, baby-cute features and a flawless complexion. There was only a hint of pale lipstick on her rather full, perfectly formed mouth. And when she caught sight of her welcoming committee, the girl flashed a brilliant white smile that added, along with her small yet voluptuous figure, to the impression that a Hollywood starlet had come to call on the Lelands.

"I nearly whizzed past the place," she called out brightly. "Do I have the right house? Miss Leland? I'm Beth de Haven."

Janet welcomed her in and introduced her to Aunt Cammie, whose expression, as she surveyed the girl's yellow-and-white-striped mini-dress, registered a cross between amazement and disapproval.

There was a breathless jumble of answers to Janet's hospitable questions: It was a sultry morning — would Beth like a cold drink?

The girl's violet-blue eyes lit up with amusement. "No, thanks, dear. I try not to booze it up before noon."

"My niece meant *lemonade*," Aunt Cammie said. Surprisingly, there was no harshness in her tone.

"I know," Beth said, winking at the older woman. "I've got a facetious tongue in my head. But no, thanks, anyway." She hadn't yet accepted Janet's invitation to sit down, pacing the long porch nervously and expressing delight with the old-fashioned glider and rocking chairs. "Hey, wow . . . this is like the old town replica at Disneyland — only it's for real! I'll have to buy some quaint threads . . . you know, like I want to fit in."

"I'm sure you will, dear," Cammie assured the girl. "We want you to feel right at home."

It was strange; Janet would have expected her aunt to disapprove of Beth's breezy manner and, certainly, of her obviously expensive but sparse attire.

Cammie was not even disturbed by the girl's casual wave at the luggage-laden Jaguar outside. "Do you want your houseboy to haul in my junk now? I'm in no rush, but I'd love to shower. . . ."

"We don't *have* a houseboy," Cammie told her. "And no maid."

Beth's grin lighted up the already sunlit porch. "Oh, how wild! A sort of do-it-yourself pad."

Cammie was eyeing the girl with an amazingly sympathetic look, considering her usual hostility toward "racy young flibbertigibbets," and, certainly, if any girl gave the impression of qualifying for that title, Beth de Haven did! "We're all responsible for our own personal belongings and our own rooms, Beth," Cammie said. She was as firm as always, but more than usually patient. "Now, if you want to pitch in, Janet and I will help you get settled."

"No maids," Beth said, more to herself than anyone else. "How neat. My folks' places in Long Island and Miami absolutely *crawl* with help. It gets to be a drag when you want a little privacy. Know what I mean?"

"We wouldn't know," Cammie told her. With Beth chirping, as though the physical process of unloading her mounds of luggage from the car were a mad adventure, Janet and her aunt got her settled in a room whose polished oak floors, flowered chintz curtains, and brass bedstead were labeled as "crazy," "wild," "groovy" and "out of sight" — all presumably expressions of enthusiasm.

After lunch, Janet and Cammie invited the girl to join them on the porch while they watched for the other boarder. Beth made her appearance, fresher than before, after a lengthy shower and a change to a white linen outfit that was, if that were possible, more revealing than the dress she had worn during the last lap of her drive from New York.

"You're sure I won't be in the way?" she asked as she plopped into the creaky glider. "I mean, if you have things to do. . . ."

"Dishes are done," Cammie said. Her big, always busy hands were occupied painting pink acrylic flowers on one of her new tongue-depressor wren houses. "Janet's day off. We planned our time so's we'd have this day to get you and the other young lady settled."

"Wow, *that's* a switch," the pretty blonde said.

Janet frowned. "A what?"

"A change from the routine I'm used to. Every time I've come home after getting bounced out of some school or other, I've had the distinct impression that I'm in the way."

"In whose way?" Janet asked.

"The mater's. Or the pater's." Beth shrugged. "Big party being planned, house guests coming, getting ready for a cruise. Always some big deal going on."

Beth lapsed into a pensive silence, and Janet caught a flicker of sadness on her face — a tragic expression that made the girl's bouncy attitude appear, suddenly, like a defensive facade. Aunt Cammie had seen it, too; she had forgotten her project and was studying Beth intently. With her typical bluntness, Cammie asked the question that Janet had only begun to mull over in her mind:

"I guess you've come from a home where you're used to having people wait on you, is that right?"

Beth nodded, but the flashing smile did not materialize. Mercifully, Cammie didn't mention the fact that rejection by her parents was also part of Beth's plush existence.

"Isn't it going to be rough for you to turn the tables?" Cammie persisted. "Being a nurse, y'know . . . that involves waiting on other people. And then some. You have to do all sorts of grisly. . . ."

"Auntie, you're going to scare Beth out of nursing before she even starts training!" Janet warned.

"I'm just being realistic," Cammie snapped.

"Honestly, girl. Whatever made you decide to become a nurse?"

Beth stared out at the elm tree in the front yard for an interminable time, her beautifully colored eyes glazed as though she were sightless. Finally, she said, "There isn't much left to try. I've flopped at everything else."

Janet resisted telling the girl that nursing was hardly a last-resort profession. It was a demanding field that required stamina and dedication, and the first year of training weeded out all but the most determined applicants. And Beth was intelligent; surely she had known this when she decided on her course! Instead, Janet asked, "Were your parents happy about your. . . ."

"They're always glad to get me out of their hair," Beth cut in. She took a cigarette from the pack that was always within easy reach. Her perfectly sculptured hands (hands that had never touched dishwater, Janet observed) trembled as she held a lighter to the cigarette. "I'm not chopping them," she said flatly. "I've been nothing but a headache to my family. Can't blame them for being overjoyed to get rid of me." Beth's sudden laughter, tinny and sardonic, sent a shiver through Janet. "You'll see. A few weeks from now, you'll be wanting me out of your cozy little pad, too. And that'll be too bad, because I could really groove here. It's like . . . the kind of house you see in old story books. All it needs is a papa with a moustachio and a plump mama in a flowered apron and. . . ."

Beth stopped short, probably noticing the nasturtium-printed cotton apron tied around Cammie's ample midsection. "Oh, I'm sorry. I wasn't being flippant. I was trying to say. . . ."

Whatever Beth de Haven was trying to say was lost as a taxi eased up to the curb behind her yellow sports car.

Minutes later, Janet was welcoming the second boarder, a drab, mousy girl who looked at least ten years older than the "18" written on her housing application.

Feature-by-feature, Phyllis Straley was not an ugly girl, but there was a sallow, hangdog look about her face. Combined with the dejected, stoop-shouldered posture of her gangling frame and her frightened, uneasy manner, the face made Janet think of weary old age. Her lusterless hair had been amateurishly tortured by curlers into a frizzly mop — Janet pictured it hanging in unattractive wisps when the home "beauty treatment" was not applied. She wore an obviously new beige blouse and matching skirt, but the blouse hung limply from her shoulders and the skirt drooped in shapeless folds.

Introductions left Phyllis breathless and awed. Her examination of Beth de Haven was that of a charlady meeting a diamond-bedecked dowager, and her only comment, when asked about the trip from her small home town in Tennessee, was a thin whine about the cost of the bus fare and the exorbitant expense of having to take a cab from the station.

22

Solicitously, Aunt Cammie heated leftovers from their lunch. Phyllis wolfed down the meal, saying, "Yes, ma'am" to Cammie's comment that she needed "fattening up."

After an awkward session, from which Beth excused herself abruptly, Phyllis revealed, under friendly questioning, that she came from a straight-laced rural community, that her parents were "poor but righteous people," and that she was fearful about "living in a fancy place like this."

Janet gathered that the girl had been raised to equate joy with sin. Apparently the old house looked luxurious to Phyllis, who was aware of her comparatively poor appearance; for she made a pathetic reference to her skimpy wardrobe and to the racks of new clothing she had glimpsed in the room next to her own.

"I'm just going to have enough to get by on," Phyllis said. Her voice, like her face, was colorless and mournful.

"What a challenge," Janet said to her aunt when their second guest had complained of tiredness and had retired to her room. "Can't you see that kid with a new hairdo and. . . ."

"And a whole new personality?" Cammie interrupted in a crisp tone.

"All she needs is some grooming advice and someone to let her know that life isn't all misery, misery, misery." Janet helped her aunt clear the wicker porch table, following her into the kitchen. "I feel awfully sorry for the girl. Beth's absolutely sure of herself, but that poor, sad little creature's going to need all the attention we can give her. We'll have to be subtle, of course. We don't want her thinking we've torn into making her over — and make her *more* self-conscious — but. . . ."

Janet stopped, aware of Cammie's unsmiling scrutiny. After a long silence, she said, "What's the matter? What did I say wrong?"

Cammie pursed her lips for a moment. Then she busied herself rinsing off Phyllis' luncheon dishes at the sink.

"Cammie? Did I say something wrong?"

There was another long pause before Janet's aunt, careful not to make her words sound like the advice she abhorred, said, "You're like your father, rest his soul. My brother Frank knew less about human nature than I know about opera. Wouldn't have known the good guys from the bad guys in a Western, but for the fancy white fringe on the hero's shirt."

"And precisely what does that have to do with my feeling sorry for. . . ."

"For the wrong girl," Cammie said.

Janet laughed. "All right, so Beth's folks have gotten fed up with her. After doing a good job of spoiling her themselves, probably. But if you think I'm going to feel sorry for that gorgeous blonde — pity the poor little rich girl — you've got it all wrong. Funny, your reactions to the two of them were exactly the opposite of what I would have expected. Lloyd talked about in-

24

viting headaches, and the minute Beth walked in, I thought. . . ."

"You thought wrong," Cammie said — and in a tone indicating that all further attempts at pursuing the subject would be wasted effort.

Janet made one final attempt anyway. "What makes you think . . . ?"

"Have to swat a few flies for my Venus's-flytraps," Cammie muttered. "I should have saved a few scraps of that ground round . . . poor things haven't been fed for days."

The discussion of their new boarders was now over, Janet knew. She returned to the porch, spending the rest of the time before dinner devising plans for bringing the ugly duckling out of her shell.

THREE

Aunt Cammie's semiprediction about which of the girls would present more problems proved inaccurate.

During their first month at the hospital-affiliated university, Beth and Phyllis seemed to face equal scholastic trials — no better and no worse than Janet remembered from her own training. Phyllis applied herself to her textbooks with dronelike persistence; Beth, though she devoted less time to study, had a quick mind and breezed through memorization of bone and muscle nomenclature with an almost indifferent airiness. Their grades, Janet guessed, would both be average.

It was on the social level that Janet's student boarders were poles apart. There were few evenings when Beth de Haven did not have a date, usually with some junior member of the Danforth Hospital's medical staff. Conversely, in spite of Janet's efforts to brighten Phyllis' drab appearance, the latter played Cinderella to Beth's role as the popular princess.

Phyllis blamed her lack of male attention on money problems. "If I had Beth's wardrobe. . . ." she would complain. Or, "If I had traveled to all kinds of expensive places like Beth, I'd be more interesting to fellows. She knows how to play tennis, and she has her own car." To these explanations, Phyllis would add a final note of righteousness: "Men don't care about girls who don't smoke or drink or carry on." At times Phyllis would bemoan her strict upbringing, but more often she would use it as a defense, insisting that "old-fashioned girls" were never rushed for dates.

"Janet doesn't smoke, drink, or 'carry on' — whatever that means," Cammie reminded the girl. "And she hasn't found that any handicap."

"Well . . . Janet's pretty," was Phyllis' glum conclusion. "And she has so many beautiful clothes. . . ."

Since Aunt Cammie refused to give advice, Janet found herself in the position of housemother: urging Beth to stop wearing herself out on late-night dates and seeking a solution to Phyllis' problem. A part-time filing job in Lloyd's office was arranged for the dour hill-country girl.

"I don't really need an extra person for filing," Lloyd said when Janet made the suggestion. "And heaven knows I can't put that bundle of gloom into the reception room. Besides, how much time can she spare from school and homework?"

"Phyllis can work all day Saturdays," Janet told him. "Please, honey. Just earning a few dollars every week will do wonders for her morale."

Phyllis was pleased with the arrangement, but

though she managed to buy several tasteless outfits after a few weeks on the job, there was no appreciable change in her appearance or attitude. Janet gave up her attempt at transforming Phyllis into a pert, attractive young woman. She was grateful that, at least, Lloyd had no complaints about the employee she had foisted on him.

"She's efficient," he commented one evening. "Knocks herself out to please, and a little on the obsequious side, but the files are in order. I didn't expect Phyllis to brighten any dark corners in the office."

Still dateless, Phyllis was a frequent member of the evening "family circle" that gathered around the Leland fireplace, as the days drifted into late October and the evenings became nippy. Another frequent member of the group that included Lloyd Turner, Phyllis, Aunt Cammie, and Janet was a twenty-two-year-old pharmacology student named Denny Reese.

Denny's home was in Danforth, though Janet had never met the plumpish young man until he came to take Beth de Haven out to a Student Union dance. With his round, rather childish blue eyes, a crop of tightly curled red hair that flopped in all directions in spite of Denny's attempts to tame it, and a direct, almost naïve manner of speaking, Denny was instantly likeable. Unfortunately, Beth de Haven did not share the rest of the household's opinion of Denny Reese, a fact that he deplored aloud one evening when he came to call on Beth, only to learn that she had gone out with an intern.

"I must be using the wrong kind of soap," he announced to anyone in the living room who might have been interested. Janet had asked him in for coffee, and Denny had accepted the invitation with boyish eagerness. Seated on the floor near Aunt Cammie's feet, halfheartedly watching her braiding a raffia belt, Denny made a minor-key whistling sound. "I dunno. Beth seemed all gung-ho to go out with me that first time. And we had a ball, too. 'Least I thought we did. She's nice enough when I see her around, and she doesn't hang up in my face or anything when I call her. But you think I can get another date? Anybody here know what I did wrong?"

Janet smiled at Denny's refreshing honesty, but she could offer no explanation.

Denny turned his attention to Aunt Cammie. "You know Beth pretty well, Miss Leland. What would you advise me to . . . ?"

Lloyd and Janet laughed, after which it was necessary to explain Cammie's policy about advice to the confused young man. Phyllis Straley was usually silent during these informal sessions between dinner and the time for Lloyd Turner's evening rounds at the hospital. Surprisingly, she spoke up now. "If you'll notice, Beth hardly ever goes out with the same fellow more than once. Two or three times at the most, but no more."

"Keep pretty close tabs on her, do you?" Aunt Cammie said.

Phyllis' normally sallow complexion colored, and tears welled up in her eyes. "I just . . . well, anybody would notice. . . ." She got up from her chair and raced out of the room.

Janet started to follow her, then turned to her aunt, half-whispering, "Cammie, was that dig necessary? You know how sensitive Phyllis is."

"I also know that people ought to mind their own business," Cammie said.

Denny looked embarrassed. "Man, did I start something! The thing is, it happens to be true. I'm not the only guy who got the brush-off after one date." He lumbered to his feet slowly. "I have a hunch why, but. . . ." Denny shrugged one shoulder, leaving the sentence hanging. "I'd like to talk to Beth about it sometime," he said after an awkward silence.

Lloyd tried to ease the tension in the room by suggesting that Beth would eventually run out of new suitors and have to start the old round again. "That should put you up right near the top of the list," he told Denny.

"In the meantime," Janet said, "feel free to drop by anytime, Denny. You're bound to catch Beth at home one of these evenings. She's got to run out of energy, if she doesn't run out of boy-friends."

"Not much chance of that," Denny said. He looked disconsolate as Janet walked him to the door. As they passed the stairwell, muffled sobs from Phyllis Straley's room added to the uneasy atmosphere.

On the porch, Denny hesitated after saying good night. Janet had the distinct impression that there was something he wanted to say, something he could not bring himself to express. Later, when they were alone, she told Lloyd about the incident, attributing the young man's behavior to lovesickness.

"I'm glad I don't have to compete with the whole intern staff and all those sharp young lab technicians," Lloyd joked. "I'd probably go around looking more miserable than Denny. And getting tongue-tied when I tried to confide in strangers." He drew Janet into his arms. "We're very lucky, darling. Sure of each other. Nobody else to worry about. None of this being eaten up by jealousy."

Janet nestled her head against his chest, nodding contentedly. "Very lucky," she echoed.

Less than a week later, the words were to become meaningless.

FOUR

It began pleasantly enough, on a Saturday afternoon when Janet stopped at Lloyd Turner's office after she got off duty — not with the
intention of seeing Lloyd, for she had just left
him at the hospital, but because it had occurred
to her that Phyllis Straley might appreciate a ride
home.

Phyllis was more than appreciative. Sitting beside Janet as they drove through the busy afternoon traffic downtown, she said, "You don't
know how grateful I am for this, Janet. I get so
tired walking home, and the buses are so unde-
pendable. I'm always glad when Beth stops for
me, except . . . you know how she drives. I'm always scared to death."

"Beth stops for you?" Janet asked the question
casually. "Come to think of it, you *did* come
home together last Saturday."

"The last three Saturdays." Phyllis paused,
and Janet sensed a sudden uneasiness. "She has
her hair done at that expensive shop just
down the street from Dr. Turner's office, so
she says it's no trouble. When I work part-time
during the week, Beth has to go out of her way to
pick me up. We have our Nutrition classes on opposite days, you know. But . . . she drives all the

way downtown from the campus and then back this way."

"Well, that's . . . very thoughtful of her," Janet said. For no reason at all she found her breathing accelerated. "I didn't know Beth had time for. . . ."

"She doesn't mind," Phyllis said quickly. "If she gets to the office before I'm finished working, she talks with Dr. Turner. I guess she told you. . . ."

"No. No, she hasn't mentioned it." Janet braked to a jarring stop at a red light, her mind occupied with another thought: Lloyd hadn't mentioned Beth's visits, either. Testily, worried about exaggerating a perfectly innocent situation, she said, "It's really not a very important subject matter, is it? I see Beth so rarely, and then she's usually in a rush to go somewhere. And I have. . . ." Janet stopped. It would have sounded too defensive to mention that she had more interesting matters to discuss with her fiancé. Instead, Janet repeated her earlier remark about Beth's "thoughtfulness."

"She didn't really go out of her way the first time," Phyllis said. Janet glanced away from the road long enough to catch a nervous twitching of the other girl's face. "The *first* time she came to the office, Beth had an appointment. It just happened that we were leaving at the same time, and I guess she felt sorry for me."

Janet ignored the self-pitying tone — Phyllis assumed that everyone viewed her as an object of

33

pity. "She had a . . . *professional* appointment?"

"Yes, didn't the doctor tell you?"

"No. Do you know . . . is there something wrong?"

"Beth didn't tell me, and I didn't see the file." Phyllis had begun her annoying habit of twisting the fingers of one hand with the others. "I don't know what Doctor did with the card — he *usually* leaves them in the slot in whatever consulting room he uses."

"I'm sure there's a good explanation," Janet said.

She regretted the irritation that had crept into her voice as Phyllis made a worried, whining sound. "Oh, dear! I hope I haven't said anything to upset you. If I've said something to cause any trouble between you and Dr. Turner, I'll just die. You've both been so wonderful to me, and Beth's been so nice about driving me home. . . ."

"No trouble. Don't be ridiculous, Phyllis. Why would there. . . ."

"It's probably just the way it looks to me." Phyllis was close to tears. "I'm so fond of you and the doctor. And Beth. . . ."

"What about Beth?" Janet asked sharply. She was having difficulty concentrating on the traffic.

"I haven't wanted to say anything about this. I wouldn't say anything in the world to hurt you, Miss Leland . . . Janet . . . you know that."

"What makes you think. . . ."

"Well, I *know* you're upset. I can see that. And

it's all my fault. I shouldn't have mentioned anything about Beth coming to the office, using me as an excuse to . . . hang around. I know she doesn't care enough about me to . . . wait around until I'm finished with work. She'd be ashamed to be seen with me around the campus, I *know* that. And the way she . . . makes up to men. She comes in looking like a million dollars, all smiles — and those flirty remarks she makes. . . ."

"Phyllis?"

The girl gasped at Janet's sharpness.

"Beth *always* looks attractive. She can't help knowing she's attractive, because she *is*. Charming men is a . . . sort of conditioned reflex with her, and I don't think you want to imply anything else. Do you? You can give her credit for sharing her car with you and being a considerate person, can't you?"

Janet cursed herself under her breath as Phyllis broke out with sniffling tears. "I did . . . exactly what I promised myself . . . I'd never do. Make trouble. I . . . didn't mean anything . . . bad."

"Then forget it," Janet ordered.

They drove the rest of the way home in silence. But if Phyllis was able to forget the conversation, Janet was haunted by it for the rest of the day. When her dinner date with Lloyd began to loom up as an uncomfortable encounter, she decided to rid herself of the ugly suspicion that had been planted in her mind by confronting Beth directly.

Trembling inside, hating herself for making an issue of something blurted out by a somewhat neurotic girl, Janet approached the subject as she passed Beth's room after dinner. The door was open, Cammie and Phyllis were still downstairs dawdling over their coffee, and Beth turned from her dresser mirror to smile. It seemed an ideal time to ask the troublesome question. Janet began cautiously: "Are you busy, Beth?"

Beth ran several quick brushstrokes through her hair as she said, "Just trying to get the snarls out of this stupid . . . mess of spaghetti. With the top down, it gets all . . . tangly."

"You're going out?"

"I guess. Fred Walsh. No. Correction. This twerpy intern . . . Bradley Somebody. Cameron. Fred's tomorrow."

"Aren't you overdoing it a little, Beth? Not that it's any of my business — heaven knows I don't want to be a prying housemother at my age, but . . . I heard you haven't been feeling well."

Beth's eyes, reflected in her dresser mirror, showed mild surprise. "I s'pose Dr. Turner told you." She turned, facing Janet without any show of evasiveness and waving her hairbrush at the bed. "Hey, you've been on your feet all day. Sit down a minute."

Janet sank down to perch on the edge of the bed, grateful that she hadn't been forced to mention Phyllis. "If you've got any kind of problem, you know the Supervisor of Nursing

Services can arrange. . . ."

"I wanted to see a private doctor," Beth said. "I mean, I can afford to pay for medical help. Not that I'm going to get any. My family's spent a bundle sending me to neurologists and what have you, but nobody's been able to do any good." In answer to Janet's questioning look, she explained, "Headaches. I get some dillies. But. . . ." Beth shrugged, and the familiar smile flashed on again. "They go away. Between times, I'm fine. No sweat."

"Did Dr. Turner . . . ?"

Beth turned back to the mirror and began a furious brushing of the long blond hair. "He couldn't do anything for me, either. Nothing against his ability, understand. I've had my head looked at by gray-bearded experts. One from Vienna, yet. Please don't worry. I've been grooving along for weeks now."

Beth's attitude was so frank that Janet found it impossible to continue the probe. When she mentioned Beth's headaches to Lloyd during their restaurant dinner that night, he was equally disarming.

"The kid came to see me . . . let's see . . . twice," Lloyd said. "Yes, she kept two appointments. I suspected there wasn't any organic reason for the severe headaches she complained about, but I suggested a complete neurological examination. Beth told me she's had dozens. Those were her words: dozens."

"But there's got to be a reason," Janet protested.

37

"Sure. One of my guesses was that the pain was psychosomatic. I got the impression Beth hasn't had a happy relationship with her family. Lots of school trouble, although she had to come up with a pretty good scholastic record to be accepted at Danforth. From what I was able to learn, she's doing average work. She's not going to be any Florence Nightingale, and she'd probably do better if she applied herself more, but the headaches weren't a cover-up for poor grades. Or lack of social acceptance."

Janet smiled. "Hardly."

"So, between visits I talked to your aunt — one evening while you were upstairs getting dressed. She told me Beth goes a mile a minute, all enthusiasm and energy. And then she has broody periods. Locked up in her room after classes. . . ."

"She gets home at one-thirty most days," Janet muttered. "I don't see her until dinnertime."

"If Cammie says she has depressive periods to go with all that manic activity, I'll take her word for it," Lloyd said. "The second time Beth came to see me, I started to suggest psychological reasons for . . . well, she called them 'excruciating' headaches."

"And?"

"And, she made some flippant remark about not needing a headshrinker and walked out. Not in anger." Lloyd frowned at his salad, apparently trying to recall the scene. "She was polite. Maybe a little condescending. I remember her saying something about my being a 'groovy guy', and telling me not to feel badly, because she'd consulted doctors who charge fees ten times higher than mine and they hadn't given her any different advice. I felt terrible about letting her go. I don't think Beth's a hypochondriac. If the headaches are genuine, she needs help."

"Can't you get her to . . . ?"

"Look, I can't rope a patient with a lasso. I told your aunt to try to get the girl to consult a psychiatrist. Cammie seems to be fairly close to the girl. Likes her. I'll feel a lot better if I know Beth's under medical care."

There was no reason to doubt Lloyd's words. Yet Janet had not freed herself completely from the rankling suspicion. "You . . . still see Beth from time to time."

"Not at your house," Lloyd said. "You know she's always gone by the time I get there. No, she comes by to give Phyllis a lift once in a while, but I haven't succeeded in having a serious talk with her. She's very clever about dodging the issue. I didn't want to worry you with the problem. She certainly doesn't look or act like a 'sick' person. I've been hoping I can resolve it one of these days when I see her in my waiting room. She usually has a ten or fifteen minute wait for . . . what's her name? Phyllis."

Except for Janet's concern over her pretty young boarder, the subject was all but dropped until a week later, when Janet returned from the hospital to find her aunt banging pots and pans in the kitchen, obviously in a surly mood and to-tally uncommunicative. Not unexpectedly, Janet heard muffled sobs from upstairs. She hurried to Phyllis Straley's room.

It took twenty minutes of coaxing before Phyllis revealed that the older woman had insti-gated the tears with harsh words.

"My aunt has a sharp tongue," Janet consoled. "But she means well. Honestly, Phyllis, if I took some of those caustic remarks of Cammie's seri-ously, I'd be in a real mess."

Phyllis lay stretched across the bed, her stringy hair plastered to her tear-stained face. "I know. She was right. I shouldn't have . . . told her . . . what I did."

There was another long period of trying to get Phyllis' sobs under control, and then Janet asked, "What did you say to Cammie, for good-ness' sake?"

"I just . . . asked her . . . advice . . . about. . . ."

Janet patted the girl's shoulder and grinned. "Oh, come on! Haven't you been here long enough to know that Cammie has a phobia about giving advice? She wouldn't give a person the time of day if she thought there was some question about it. Look, if you want advice, ask me. I *love* telling other people what to do. *Every-body* does. Everybody except. . . ."

"I . . . can't talk to you about it," Phyllis choked. "I asked . . . *her* about what to do, be-cause . . . I didn't want to hurt you. But I . . . didn't want people sneaking around behind your back. And . . . I thought, maybe you'll get hurt anyway, so maybe you should know. . . ."

"Know *what?*" Janet demanded. For some unaccountable reason her palms felt clammy and her heart had begun an erratic thumping.

Phyllis covered her face with her scrawny hands. "No one's ever been as kind to me as you. I wish I could die! It's so awful, and I had to ask somebody what to do. And . . . she *yelled* at me. She was so. . . ."

"Phyllis, will you please tell me what you're talking about?"

"Beth," Phyllis whispered. "She's gone out in her own car three times this week. She . . . said she had dates, but . . . she couldn't even remember the names of . . . these fellows she claimed she was going to meet. And . . . I knew you were looking forward to seeing that . . . Italian movie with Dr. Turner."

"Yes?"

"And then he called and said he had an emergency at the hospital."

"Phyllis, I happen to know. . . ."

"He *did* have an emergency case," Phyllis cried. "But he wasn't at the hospital all evening. I . . . took the bus downtown that night because I had to buy this . . . special notebook paper. I had an assignment to do, and the stationery store on Osborne Street was closed, so I remembered the downtown stores were open on Thursday nights. . . ."

"Phyllis, will you . . . ?"

"I saw them together! Beth and Dr. Turner. They were parked over near the square, sitting in her car. They didn't see me, but I saw *them,* and I know they've been having these secret meetings." Phyllis turned her face to the wall, sobs racking her thin body. "I haven't been able to sleep. I didn't know what to do. Then, when I came home today, I thought . . . I thought if I asked . . . somebody else who loves you. . . ."

There were no more words left inside Phyllis. Janet's misery was almost secondary to that of the pathetic creature she had tried, unsuccessfully, to help. There was nothing to do but assure Phyllis that she had done nothing wrong, to apologize for Aunt Cammie's angry outburst, and to thank the girl for her loyalty.

After that, it was Janet's turn to cry.

FIVE

"I told you I had an emergency case that night, because I *had* an emergency case!" Lloyd fumed. "A genuine, bona fide red blanket. If you want to check with Admitting, you'll learn that he had to be pried out of his car and it took from six o'clock until almost nine to put him back together again. Ted Frawley. He's recuperating in 309, if your suspicious little mind still isn't satisfied."

"There's no need to get nasty," Janet protested.

Danforth Hospital's staff dining room was hardly the place for a lovers' quarrel. Several nurses seated at an adjoining table were making polite but unsuccessful efforts not to stare, and Janet wished she had kept silent about Lloyd's rendezvous with Beth until there was more privacy. But, then, she hadn't realized that Lloyd's reaction would be so severe.

"If I have to be checked up on like a criminal," he was saying angrily, "forget it! You don't want to marry a man you don't trust. And, let me assure you, I want a wife, not a watchdog. Not someone who takes the word of some . . . unnamed gossip against mine."

"You haven't denied that you were out with. . . ."

43

"I wasn't out with anybody!" Lloyd cried out.

Janet felt her face coloring. "Lloyd, please! People are. . . ."

"I don't care what other people are doing — I care about *us*." In spite of his protest, Lloyd lowered his voice — though his fury was still visible. "I resent even having to explain something as trivial as . . . talking to a girl I saw twice as a patient, a patient I've worried about. When I finished in Surgery that night, I stopped at Harger's craft shop to pick up a new kind of epoxy glue your aunt said she'd like to try. I knew it was too late for the movie, but I figured on stopping at your place anyway."

"But you just *happened* to run into Beth de Haven."

Janet's sarcastic tone set off a fresh explosion. "*Yes!* I just *happened* to run into Beth de Haven! She was walking down Main Street in a daze. Couldn't remember where she had parked her car, couldn't find her keys, didn't know where she had been or where she was going. And her head hurt, she told me. I helped her locate the car, over by the square, but I didn't think she was in any condition to drive."

"Had she been drinking?" Janet's tone remained caustic and incredulous.

"She looked ill. I didn't care *how* she'd gotten that way." Lloyd dropped his fork to the table with a clatter that invited more stares from the nurses at the next table. "What I'm saying is that I didn't take time for a moral lecture. I sat down

44

with her and tried to talk her into letting me drive her to the hospital. I didn't get anywhere. She seemed better after awhile, and I got her to promise to come in and see me at the office the next day."

"I'm sure she did," Janet said.

"As a matter of fact, she *didn't*." Lloyd looked around the crowded dining room as though he were looking for a means of escape. "I think I've diagnosed her problem. As soon as I can confirm my suspicions, drastic action's going to be needed. It could be serious."

"I suppose that's why you told me all about it," Janet persisted sarcastically. "Beth lives in my home. I have *some* responsibility for her. If you were that worried. . . ."

"Look, I've already told you that I promised the kid I wouldn't break her confidence. I'm a doctor, Janet, not a tattletale. Beth was afraid you'd ask her to leave — send her back to her parents — if you thought something was seriously wrong. I insisted on following her home in my car, but I had to promise not to tell you. . . ."

"I didn't know we kept secrets from each other." Janet's hurt resentment had not been appeased, even though Lloyd's explanation rang true. "I can respect your professional ethics, but when you hold your consultations in a car that belongs to a girl who. . . ."

Lloyd crumbled his napkin and threw it down on the table. "I've violated enough professional rules trying to explain a perfectly innocent encounter. That's not the point. It's *having* to account for myself that sickens me."

"In other words, I'm not supposed to know about it when you. . . ."

"Lending me money doesn't mean you own me," Lloyd cut in. "If I had borrowed that ten thousand from the bank the way I wanted to, I wouldn't have to report to the board of directors everytime I ran across someone who needed help!"

"Money has nothing to do with it," Janet snapped. "It was the underhanded. . . ."

Lloyd got to his feet hurriedly, his face blanched. "I don't want to hear anymore! Apparently you trust me with ugly misfits when they need a hand. Beth's principal offense is being attractive. Right? Married to you, I'd have to specialize in ugly women, preferably past their sixties. I'm a doctor, Janet. I'm not your puppet, and I'm not going to become one for ten grand." Too furious to be embarrassed by his audience, Lloyd turned away from the table. "I'll see that you're repaid," he said.

"And I'll see that you get your ring," Janet cried.

Lloyd couldn't have heard her; he was pounding his heels in a disgusted stride toward the door.

Left to face the humiliating glances of every staff member within earshot, Janet forced herself to finish her coffee, trying to pretend that the scene had meant nothing to her. No one, she

46

hoped, was noticing that her hand shook so se-
verely that her coffee spilled over into the saucer
as she tried to lift the cup.

A tortured eternity later, she made her way out
of the dining hall, sick with the realization that it
was all over. Her engagement to Lloyd, the wonderful wedding plans, the happy prospects for
the future . . . all finished. It was incomprehen-
sible, especially the fact that she had triggered
the disgraceful argument herself.

Janet returned to her duties, going through the
motions of caring for her patients with the dead-
ened motions of a zombi, shutting out of her
mind the possibility that Lloyd had been right
and she had been wrong — completely wrong.
There was only one avenue of escape from heart-
break, and that was to cling to righteous indigna-
tion, pretending that the blame was entirely
Lloyd's. It was a slim thread; Janet held onto it,
however, throughout the day, saving honest
misery for a time when no one would see her
tears.

SIX

It was impossible to keep the broken engagement a secret from Aunt Cammie, of course. Or, for that matter, from the other two occupants of the Leland household; Lloyd Turner was more than conspicuous by his absence, and Janet gave up trying to conceal her ringless finger.

Beth made no comment, either out of discretion or because she was too busy on her social merry-go-round to notice that Janet was spending all her evenings at home. If Janet's attitude toward the girl was sometimes chilly and sometimes overly solicitous (for remembering Lloyd's concern and seeing Beth's pallor disturbed Janet's conscience), Beth seemed blithely unaware of any change in their relationship. When she was not rushing off to school or on a date, she was usually secluded in her room. Janet assumed that she was studying, and perhaps Beth read too much; more often than not the lovely violet-blue eyes were veiled by a dull, unseeing expression.

There was no sympathy forthcoming from Aunt Cammie. "I didn't advise you to fall in love with Dr. Turner," she said one morning, "and I didn't advise you to send back his engagement ring. Whatever you've done, you've done without any influence from me. I've got to assume that you did precisely what you wanted to do, Janet."

Janet's protest that this cold, objective attitude was almost inhuman, brought a stony silence from her aunt. Cammie made only one additional comment: "Nothing good ever comes from taking a viper to your bosom." Janet considered this reference to Beth de Haven a trifle strong, but she gave up trying to pump any consolation from the woman who had raised her.

Only Phyllis was sympathetic, and her consolations were so emotional that Janet almost preferred Cammie's policy of noninvolvement. "I know what it's like to be alone," Phyllis said. "At least you know you won't be alone long. You'll find somebody else."

Janet disagreed; she wasn't interested in other men. In an overwrought moment she admitted to Phyllis that she "probably" still loved Lloyd Turner. Still, there was some reassurance in knowing that rejection by Lloyd had not condemned her to a life of spinsterhood. It was hard to feel sorry for yourself when you were exposed to Phyllis Straley's misery. For Janet, at least, there was the hope of finding love again.

Richard Wexton did not represent love, and certainly not love at first sight. Janet's first encounter with the new internist on the Danforth Hospital staff was hardly a breathtaking experience. He was entirely too fresh and too personal, Janet thought, and too conscious of his rather suave, handsome appearance.

Slim and wiry, his slender face crowned by wavy golden-yellow hair and embellished by a meticulously groomed, pencil-thin, almost colorless moustache, Dr. Wexler had earned a quick reputation, among the single nurses, as a "wolf."

"He doesn't waste any time," was the general consensus of opinion. One of the nurses on Janet's ward said that the new doctor's hazel eyes didn't just look at you — they took a "constant inventory." There was mixed admiration and ridicule of Richard Wexton's sophisticated, if somewhat flashy wardrobe; certainly he dressed more like a continental movie actor than an Ohio university town medic. Yet Janet noticed that the more snide remarks were made by nurses the bachelor doctor hadn't even tried to date. And even more embittered were those who had gone out with Dr. Wexton once and hadn't been invited a second time.

In less than three weeks, the internist had become a challenge, and, in spite of her resentment (she had never before been called "sweetheart" during her first meeting with a staff M.D.!), Janet's reserve broke down. The fourth time Dr. Wexton asked her out to dinner she accepted the date.

She didn't expect to enjoy herself. Actually, Janet hoped that word would get back to Lloyd Turner via the hospital grapevine and that jealousy would cause Lloyd to end the icy politeness that passed between them now when they met in the hospital corridors, or when Janet was assigned to one of her former fiancé's patients. Besides, going out with Dr. Wexton was better than staying at home and discussing baseball heroes with Aunt Cammie or listening to Phyllis recount her misfortunes.

Rick Wexton (for he insisted upon being called Rick minutes after his slick black Continental pulled up in front of Janet's old frame house) proved to be more than just a means of filling an evening and inciting jealousy in Lloyd. He had a fantastic sense of humor that had Janet convulsed with laughter before they reached their first destination, a restaurant frequented by the sharper students and faculty members from the university. (Janet recalled dining with Lloyd at the sedate Danforth Inn, where the atmosphere was perpetually hushed.) A jazz concert followed, during which Rick revealed himself as a "hip Hippocrates." By the time they broke into the smoky clamor of the town's only discothèque, Janet had caught Rick's contagious enthusiasm for swinging evenings, and, through a cocktail-inspired haze, she recalled Lloyd as an overly serious, perhaps even dull memory from the past.

"Fun?" Rick asked when the Continental purred to a stop at Janet's curb. It was two-forty in the morning.

"I had a wonderful time," she said. "I haven't felt so alive in years."

Rick reached forward to turn down the thumping rock music that poured from the car's radio. "Who'd have thought I'd be saying the same thing in little ole Danforth? You know, I only came here because I wanted to observe some of Dr. Ainsley's diagnostic techniques. Socially, I expected to be bored to death — after New York."

"And you're not disappointed?"

Rick smiled. In the soft amber light, his face looked extraordinarily handsome. The undisguised approval in his eyes stirred an alien excitement inside Janet. "Disappointed? Darling, I just told you I came here for professional reasons. And I make it a point not to talk medicine once I peel off the white jacket. For the record, I'm getting exactly the experience I want at the hospital, and I've gotten an extra added bonus."

"Oh?"

"Meeting you. I don't have to tell you you're adorable, Janet. You've heard that before. You were delightful tonight. Hard to believe you were on the verge of settling down to the pots-and-pans routine with. . . ." Rick hesitated. "No offense, but I understand Lloyd Turner is somewhat on the square and somber side."

"He's . . . very serious about his work."

"What good doctor isn't?" Rick's forefinger tilted Janet's face upward. "I just don't believe in carrying my stethoscope out on dates. Not when

52

there's fun to be had. Not when I'm lucky enough to have a beautiful girl beside me. *This* beautiful girl. . . ."

There was no time to decide whether or not she wanted to be kissed. As Rick's arms closed around her, Janet let herself ride with the easygoing warmth of the moment, letting the eager lips close over her own in an expert kiss.

After a long time, Janet disengaged herself from the powerful embrace, realizing that her fluttering sensation was purely physical — that the only emotion she felt was a sense of shock at finding herself being kissed by a virtual stranger.

"I'd . . . rather you didn't," Janet whispered.

Rick was unoffended. "Am I rushing you? Sorry. Just so I haven't closed the door completely."

When he asked if she were free on the following Saturday night, Janet had a moment to reflect that she *was* free — free every evening of the week, and would probably remain so if she didn't forget about Lloyd. She had enjoyed the evening. Rick had understood her reaction to the premature kiss. Wouldn't it be senseless to go on nurturing a love that was dead when Rick had opened the doors to a less lonely, more enjoyable life?

"I hear they've booked a terrific band for the dance at the college Saturday. What can you lose?"

Rick's charm and self-confidence were irresistible. Janet smiled, shrugging her shoulders playfully. "You're right. What can I lose?"

She parted from Rick Wexton in a light, carefree mood, not daring to let herself remember what had already been lost.

SEVEN

Unlike Lloyd, Rick Wexton was not interested in joining the casual evenings at home in the Leland household. Although he did not say so, he obviously viewed Aunt Cammie as a ridiculous eccentric. Cammie's only response was to ignore the doctor completely.

The fourth time Rick called for Janet — anxious to get out to "where the action is" — he made the faux pas of snickering derisively at a plastic pot of beadwork flowers Cammie had painstakingly assembled from a craft kit. It was true that he hadn't known that this garish objet d'art was Cammie's handiwork, and he tried to make up for the error by lavishing extravagant praise on an equally dreadful paint-by-the-numbers portrait of an Indian warrior, also Cammie's proud effort. But after that, Janet's aunt made it a point to avoid "that Dr. Wexton" as though he were a carrier of the black plague, and Janet did her best to be ready to leave the house the moment her new admirer arrived.

She was waiting in the living room on the Sunday afternoon they had set aside for a few games of tennis, ready to leave the moment Rick arrived. He had barely walked into the room when Janet was startled by a shrill cry from the kitchen, where Phyllis and Beth were relieving Aunt Cammie of her dishwashing chore.

Rick raised his eyebrows in a barely perceptible reaction to the angry outcry. Janet flushed, murmured "excuse me just a second," and started for the kitchen. She nearly collided with Phyllis Straley as the latter came running into the dining room.

"Tell her to stop torturing me!" Phyllis cried. "Oh, Janet, how can people be so cruel?"

Janet found herself smothered in a sobbing embrace, patting Phyllis' shoulder, and asking what was wrong.

"It's Beth. She's saying awful things about me!" Phyllis wept. "She's been . . . acting so strangely all morning. You . . . you saw her during dinner. . . ."

Janet frowned, remembering the beautiful blonde's vacant stare when words were addressed to her and feeling the nervous trembling of Beth's hands. "Maybe she isn't feeling well," Janet said quietly. She was embarrassingly aware of Rick Wexton's presence just outside the dining room door. "It couldn't have been that bad." Janet untangled herself from the pathetic girl's grip. "Come on, now, Phyllis. Pull yourself together. I'm sure Beth didn't mean. . . ."

"I meant *exact*-ly pre-*cise*-ly what I said!"

Janet spun around to see Beth in the kitchen doorway. The glassy-eyed look was still there, but, unlike that of Phyllis, Beth's face was not distorted by emotion. She fixed Phyllis with a cool, level stare, and, without raising her voice — as easily as if she had been requesting cream for her coffee — Beth said, "I said you were a vicious little misfit, and that I'd just as soon live in a nest of scorpions as under the same roof with you. Unquote." Unbelievably, Beth turned on her brilliant smile. This time, however, there was a frightening quality about it, reminiscent of smiles Janet had observed during her brief training in a psychiatric ward.

Janet suppressed a gasp, determined to prevent another scene from erupting. "I'm sure you'll want to apologize for that, Beth. Phyllis is very sensitive, and. . . ."

"And so is a rattlesnake," Beth said. Her calm, under the circumstances, was eerie; Phyllis was crying pitifully and shaking her head back and forth in disbelief. "If you expect me to say I'm sorry, Janet, I'd better start packing my bags."

Janet had begun shaking inwardly. Phyllis' misery tore at her sympathy, and she realized that no amount of pity for Beth's physical or mental problems, whatever they might be, excused her behavior. It was as though Beth felt no compassion for Phyllis, as though she lacked the ability to make a comparison between herself and the tearful, ill-at-ease country girl who looked dowdy beside her — and knew it. Fighting to keep her voice under control, but furious, Janet said, "That might be the best plan, Beth. I don't intend to tolerate scenes like this. Phyllis is as much a guest in this house as you are. You've used some inexcusable. . . ."

"I said Phyllis is vicious, and she is," Beth said in a bland tone. "If you want me to get out, I can be out of here in fifteen minutes."

"I don't want any trouble," Phyllis cried. "If she'd just stop treating me like dirt! Telling me I'm a . . . I'm a horrible freak of nature."

"Did you say that?" Janet demanded.

Beth nodded slowly, directing a poisonously sweet smile at Phyllis. "I calls 'em as I sees 'em," she said.

Janet lowered her eyes. "I think you'd better make other housing arrangements, Beth. I don't like to do this, but . . . you can see that this isn't going to work out."

"Don't apologize," Beth said. She brushed her long hair back from her forehead, her hand resting there for a prolonged moment. "I've been asked to leave other people's houses before. Some I'd lived in a lot longer than this one. A few I used to call home."

Phyllis stopped crying and was staring at the other girl's unperturbed face. "Maybe she *is* sick," Phyllis whispered.

Janet felt a moment of panic, Lloyd's concern for the lovely girl prodding her conscience. "If I were you, Beth. . . ."

"You'd see a headshrinker," Beth said lightly. She brushed past Phyllis on her way to the stairwell, passing Rick Wexton without, apparently, seeing him. "Fifteen minutes," she said.

Janet was breathing hard, confusion tormenting her. If Beth was really ill. . . .

Cammie had materialized from the kitchen. She had evidently been out on the service porch, and her blazing eyes indicated she had been listening, yet she said nothing as she plodded into the dining room.

"Beth. . . ." Janet faltered under her aunt's disapproving stare.

"I heard," Cammie said. Her glance swept over Phyllis. "I suppose the least I can do is help with the packing."

"I don't know if. . . ." Janet moved forward to interrupt her aunt's stride across the room. "Maybe I didn't handle the situation as well as I could have. Beth said some outrageous things, but I hate to have her feel that we. . . . Well, you know the school won't let her stay anywhere but in an approved home, and there aren't any vacancies now. She can't go to a hotel. Maybe if you talked to her. . . ."

"Talk to her about what?" Cammie said coldly.

"I'm not sure it's right for her to leave," Janet managed to say. "Do you think I should . . . ?"

"I don't do other people's thinking for them." Cammie traced Beth's course out of the room and up the stairs. She, too, ignored Dr. Wexton.

Typically, Phyllis covered her face with her hands and ran toward a private refuge, in this case the service porch. Janet sighed and rejoined Rick in the living room, her face burning. "I'm sorry," she said. "That wasn't very pleasant."

Janet was about to ask if Rick would mind if

she cancelled their date; with everyone in the house upset, this was hardly the time to run off for a jolly afternoon at the tennis court. Rick didn't give her a chance. "They're all big people," he said casually. "They'll work out their silly little tiff. Let's go, honey. You're too young and beautiful to waste time babying a houseful of kooks."

Janet accompanied him reluctantly, worried about the emotional tangle she was leaving behind her and torn by responsibility. Less than halfway to the Danforth Country Club, where Rick was already a member in good standing, she said, "It's not fair to expect you to put up with the mood I'm in, Rick. I won't be any fun, wondering about. . . ."

"About what's going on back at your house?" Rick took his right hand from the wheel and draped it over Janet's shoulders, giving her a reassuring squeeze. "You aren't anybody's mother, sweetheart. The stringy-haired girl's going to be a mess no matter what you do. Your aunt looks like she could manage a nest of hornets with one flick of her eyelashes."

"It's *Beth* I'm worried about."

"From my observations, she's way beyond your ability to handle," Rick said. He drove along the country road for a few seconds in thoughtful silence before he concluded, "I don't like to make snap diagnoses, but I've seen that girl's symptoms before. About all you can do for her is get her to a good M.D."

"She's . . . been under medical care," Janet said. Once again, her heart began pounding erratically. "You don't mean a . . . psychiatrist, Rick?"

He shook his head. "Depends what she's on and how addicted she is to . . . whatever it is."

Janet closed her eyes for a moment, her voice barely audible as she asked the question: "Drugs?"

"I told you I don't make medical judgments after one glance at the patient. I'm just guessing," Rick said. "In any case, you're asking for nothing but trouble if you take on a responsibility like that. I'd phone the girl's family if I were you. And then I'd forget it." Rick's grip tightened around Janet. "You've got a life of your own to lead, Janet. Start living it." Janet was pulled closer to the driver, and Rick's voice was husky with affection as he murmured, "With me, darling. With me."

EIGHT

Janet returned to the house with an oppressive feeling in her chest, not unlike the suspenseful sensation she experienced every time she returned to the room of a terminal patient after a day's absence.

She had been apprehensive all afternoon. Although the weather was unseasonably warm for the first of December, the joyless, mechanical sets of tennis had left her breathless and chilled. She had begged off having dinner with Rick, yet he had insisted that Janet "warm up and relax" over hot toddies in the club's barroom. A group of his friends had drifted in, making escape more difficult. Janet had been forced to suffer through country club small talk until nearly eight o'clock, and, even then, Rick had had to be persuaded — still protesting — to drive her home.

There was no one in the living room. Janet checked the other rooms on the first floor, then crept up the stairs, wondering what it was that made her instinctively quiet, as though someone in the house was ill or asleep.

A quick glance into Beth's room told Janet that the girl was gone. Not just out on a date; the room was stripped of Beth's possessions. Strangely apprehensive, Janet walked down the hall, finding the door to Phyllis' room wide open. Phyllis was lying across her bed, wide awake, but in a deep state of depression.

"Your aunt won't even speak to me," Phyllis muttered. "She blamed *me!* Honestly, Janet, I didn't want Beth to be . . . to have to leave. If I had known this would happen, I wouldn't have let you know what she said to me. Such awful things! I couldn't take any more, and I. . . ."

"Don't blame yourself," Janet said. She felt lifeless and depressed herself, in no mood to console anyone else, yet she disliked seeing an already lonely creature agonized by guilt. "Beth hasn't been herself. We'll get her to come back and apologize, and. . . ."

"I don't think she will," Phyllis said. "She . . . *scared* me, Janet! She didn't act the way other people do when they hate somebody. All the while we were doing the dishes, she kept saying things about me that I . . . I couldn't begin to repeat. But she didn't look mad, or yell, or. . . ." Phyllis shuddered. "I was terrified. And now your aunt . . . one of the few friends I thought I had in this world. . . ."

"I'll talk to her," Janet said. She hurried out of the room before she could be subjected to another deluge of tears.

Aunt Cammie was finally located in the basement fruit cellar, furiously slapping gobs of chrome yellow paint on the wooden shelves which usually held her homemade preserves. Moving all the jars had been a gargantuan task, and the shelves had been painted only last May. Janet stepped into the small cubicle, making the first inane remark that came to mind: "You're certainly keeping yourself busy. Hi! I didn't think those shelves needed painting this soon."

"They don't." Terse-lipped, without interrupting her slapdash efforts, Cammie added, "I always find a big job for myself when I'm in this mood."

"Angry?" Janet asked softly. "I'm sorry, Aunt Cammie. Maybe I made a mistake. Do you know where Beth's gone?"

"She didn't say."

"She had to have a destination. Didn't she leave a forwarding address?"

"Didn't leave anything."

"But . . . even if she doesn't come back, she'll have to get her mail. Her money from her folks. . . ."

"I didn't pry. She said she wanted to go, and I guess she knew more about her own business than I do." Cammie kept her back turned, but her shaky voice revealed that she was far from unconcerned. "Stand back, Janet. You'll get paint on that new white outfit, and you'll have to go out and spend good money next time your doctor friend invites you out to play tennis with the swells."

Janet had forgotten that her aunt considered every sport except baseball an occupation for snobs. Normally, she would have found the remark amusing. Now, disturbed by Cammie's obvious disapproval, she said, "You didn't like my asking Beth to leave, did you? I was upset and I didn't know what to do. Phyllis was. . . ."

"The doorbell," Cammie said sharply.

"What?"

"Go see who's at the door."

Janet hadn't heard the first ring. It was repeated now, ending the awkward dialogue, with the problem still unresolved.

Their Sunday night caller was Denny Reese, and Janet was placed in the uncomfortable position of having to explain what had happened, leaving out details of the quarrel and berating herself again for having mishandled the situation. She was unprepared for the red-haired young man's shock.

"I'm not blaming you, understand," Denny said. His round blue eyes reflected a worry that seemed inconsistent with the situation; after all, roommates on the campus argued, moved out in a huff, and patched their differences often enough so that Beth's departure should not have struck Denny as a tragedy. Still, he had begun a restless pacing of the living room, his youthful face clouded as he emphasized, "I can't blame you. When Beth gets stubborn about something, there's no way to make her change her mind. I ought to know." He sighed heavily. "I tried to talk some sense into her. Get her to. . . ."

"To what?" Janet wanted to know.

Denny looked confused for a moment, then said hastily, "You know what I mean. I tried to get her to go out with me again. I really *care* about Beth, Janet. I really. . . ."

"It's all right to say you're in love with her," Janet said.

Denny was silent. After a long pause, he said, "I didn't know it was that obvious. I am. I'd do anything to be able to. . . ." Denny had started to say "help her." Evidently he decided that he had revealed too much already, the sentence ending with a disconsolate gesture.

"Do you want to try calling the hotels?" Janet asked. "She's bound to be at one of. . . ."

Janet stopped, following Denny's glance in the direction of the staircase. The sound of slow, dragging footsteps preceded Phyllis Straley's appearance.

Phyllis came into the living room as she always did, apologizing because she had "interrupted," offering to go back to her room and not "disturb," and looking as though she knew, positively, that the others were *hoping* she would leave. With her ungainly body wrapped in a faded rose-colored kimono and her eyes swollen from crying, Phyllis contributed no cheer to the glum atmosphere.

"If I told Beth it was my fault," Phyllis offered, "maybe she'd change her mind. That is, if it's all right with you, Janet."

"It would be all right until the next blow-up," Janet said. "Still, I hate to think of her being ill and alone, thinking we're all against her."

"I know the names of some of her friends,"

Phyllis said. "We could look for her at Lora Page's house. She lives with her family. Beth might have gone there."

It struck Janet that Phyllis was being too solicitous, considering Beth's attack upon her. Was she looking for an excuse to go out searching with Denny Reese? Denny had been rejected by Beth de Haven. If he realized that physical beauty was no substitute for loyalty, and if Phyllis, with a little encouragement, made an effort to make herself more attractive. . . .

"Would you be able to show Denny where this Page girl lives?" Janet asked.

Phyllis nodded.

"Why don't you get dressed, and. . . ."

"Never mind," Denny interrupted. "I can find Lora's place, and I can locate the few other girls Beth knows. There aren't that many." He started for the door, looking anxious to escape. "Thanks, anyway."

"Check back with me later," Janet told him. "I'll phone the hotels."

Denny thanked her, nodded at Phyllis, and raced out of the house.

"That's the way everybody feels about me," Phyllis moaned as soon as Denny was gone. "You meant well, I know, trying to get Denny interested in me. . . ."

Janet's protest was weak. "I didn't. . . ."

"Well, you tried to fix it up so that we'd go out together and maybe get to know each other." Phyllis was more perceptive than Janet had imagined. "That's very kind of you. I know you feel sorry for me, but . . . it's even worse when . . . you . . . when it's so plain that a fellow doesn't want anything to do with me."

"Denny's a little nervous," Janet said. "It wasn't a matter of not liking you, at all." More truthfully, she added, "I guess he's terribly fond of Beth and he's worried about her."

Phyllis sank down to the edge of the sofa, twisting her fingers as she talked. "Beth's the kind that men like. My mother was right. Decent girls don't have a chance."

"Oh, I wouldn't say that. Beth isn't just beautiful. She's full of fun, usually, and she's never depressing, never feels sorry for herself. . . ."

Phyllis was staring at the rug, her expression grim. "I'd be full of fun, too, if I was as lucky as Beth is." She looked up suddenly. "Look at *you*. You're a lot better looking than I am. You're not miserable. Dr. Turner used to like you. But look what happened. A flashy tramp comes along and . . . you're thrown over."

"It wasn't exactly like that," Janet said.

"You'd still be engaged to Dr. Turner if it hadn't been for Beth! Oh, I know she has some kind of problem and I'm willing to forgive her, but. . . ." Phyllis' face had become a rigid mask, bitterness etched into every line. "I can't forgive what she did to you, Janet. For all we know, she drove straight to Dr. Turner's apartment, and she's there right now."

NINE

Wherever the "flashy tramp" had gone that night, she was not located. When Janet saw Beth de Haven again, it was on a gurney outside of Emergency Service at Danforth Hospital.

Janet was checking out at the third floor charge desk shortly after three o'clock on Monday afternoon, when Bill Simms, one of the interns, got off the elevator and crossed over to the nurses' station. Bill looked pale and shaken. "My God, you'd think I'd be inured by now," he said. "I just saw them wheeling that girl into Emergency and I came close to passing out."

"Accident?" Janet asked.

The intern made a shuddering motion. "You'd better get down there, Janet. It's your little boarder." He apologized for breaking the news so inconsiderately. "I'm sorry. It's really thrown me. Beth . . . she's got to be the most gorgeous girl I ever went out with, and now she. . . ."

"Beth?" Janet nearly screamed at him. "What's happened?"

"They say she crashed her Jaguar into a tree out on Burdon Road. Telescoped the car. It's bad, Janet. They've got a call out for Dr. Turner . . . he's on her school record as her private physician."

Janet clutched the edge of the desk for support. "*How* bad, Bill?"

He turned away, shielding his palled young face from Janet's view. "I . . . didn't recognize her face," he said. "I only knew it was Beth because one of the nurses told me." Bill mumbled something about being wanted in Surgery and hurried away, shaking his head as though trying to shake off the horror he had just witnessed.

Janet's elevator ride to the first-floor level was a suspense-filled nightmare that was not mitigated by a tortured conscience. If Beth had been allowed to remain at the house, this would not have happened. Was the crash deliberate? Had Beth reached the end in a long series of rejections?

The dread of not knowing Beth's condition continued outside Emergency Room Two, which was closed to everyone except the taciturn doctors and nurses who raced into the room, none of them emerging.

A full hour had dragged by before a rolling stretcher was pushed through the swinging doors, with two nurses and an intern in attendance. Janet rushed to the side of the gurney, seeing Lloyd Turner's grim face before she glimpsed that of his patient.

Janet's first sight of Beth was like a stunning blow to her insides. The girl's face was cut and bruised beyond recognition. The wounds had been treated and dressed, but only a miracle of plastic surgery would recall Beth's perfect beauty. One of the nurses held a bottle from which blood poured into a vein in Beth's arm through an intravenous needle. She was obviously in shock, if not in a death coma. Janet caught her breath. "Dr. Turner . . . how badly . . . ?"

Lloyd's reply was not unsympathetic, but it was terse. "She's suffered severe head trauma, apart from the lacerations. No internal injuries that require surgery. The impact was all above her shoulders." Lloyd made his report in a mechanical monotone, as though he might be reporting to a stranger. "If you'll excuse me, I want to see her to the Intensive Care Unit."

Janet blinked back tears. "Her parents. . . ."

"They've been notified," Lloyd said. He moved on, following Beth's unconscious form to the elevator well.

Janet was watching the gurney as it moved down the long corridor on its journey to the I.C.U., when one of the Emergency Room nurses stepped out into the anteroom. She was a dour, middle-aged R.N. with whom Janet had only a casual acquaintance. "Terrible, isn't it?" the woman asked. "These kids and their cars! One of the ambulance fellas told me she must have been going ninety-five when she hit that tree. Miracle her body wasn't mangled."

"Was she alone, Mrs. Dodd?" Janet asked. Somehow she assumed the answer; in spite of Beth's popularity, it seemed now that she had always been completely alone.

71

The nurse nodded. "Yes, alone. I'd hate to have seen anybody sitting next to the driver's seat. Those are always the worst. What gets into these kids? . . . bored, rich. . . . Probably don't have anything better to do."

"Beth was studying to be a nurse," Janet said absently.

Mrs. Dodd had started fishing for a cigarette in her handbag; she was evidently on her coffee break. "Did you know her?"

More to herself than in answer, Janet said, "I don't think anyone's ever known her."

"I sure feel sorry for her parents," the other nurse said. "I can read a doctor's face like a book. You learn to do that in there." She gestured toward the Emergency Room with the unlighted cigarette. "There wasn't any skull fracture, nothing they can do for the girl in Surgery, but I could see — just from looking at Dr. Turner — that he doesn't give her a prayer."

Mrs. Dodd was walking toward the first floor nurses' lounge, anxious to light her cigarette, as she said, "You can almost smell it, sometimes. Even when they aren't hurt too badly, you kind of sense that their time is up."

TEN

Janet had never seen Aunt Cammie cry before. In the waiting room outside of the Intensive Care Unit, the plump woman who had always derided "mushy sentimentality" wept like a child when Lloyd revealed, late that night, that neither he nor the other doctors he had consulted could offer any encouragement. Beth remained in a coma. Mrs. Dodd's thoughtless prediction that the lovely girl's "time had come" hovered over the doctors and nurses who fought to save her life; no one held out hope.

Still weeping openly, Cammie was urged to take a cab home sometime near midnight. "I'll phone you if there's any change," Janet promised. "There's nothing you can do for Beth here."

Cammie nodded, wordless. She seemed to understand why Janet, who was equally powerless to help, could not leave. There were no changes by two-fifteen in the morning, when Mr. and Mrs. de Haven arrived. Oddly, although they had flown in from opposite directions, they had reached the Danforth airport at almost the same hour and had met in the hospital's main floor waiting room.

Harried, but elegantly dressed, Mrs. de Haven

had been enjoying a vacation at Miami Beach when the distressing news had reached her. Beth's father had been called back from a business trip somewhere in the East. Moments after she had introduced herself and expressed her regrets, Janet found herself disliking the couple as much as she pitied them.

Beth's mother, looking dissipated in spite of a deep Florida tan, a chic coiffure, and expertly applied, if excessive makeup, looked incapable of anything but self-gratification. At one time she had undoubtedly resembled Beth, but now the violet-blue eyes appeared hardened, and the blond hair had been tinted in a futile race against time. Pouches under her eyes and a general flabbiness gave the lie to Mrs. de Haven's attempts to cling to her fading youth. Chain-smoking, balancing her overweight body on spike-heeled pumps as she paced the marble-floored waiting room, she seemed more irritated than grieved, though Janet sensed that she was competing with her husband in a display of "sincere" concern.

Mr. de Haven was easily her match. Bald, paunchy, chewing irritably on a dead cigar, he peered at every nurse who passed the charge desk over thick-rimmed glasses, his expression indicating that no one but he was doing what should be done. Gruff and dyspeptic, he impressed Janet as the sort of person Cammie labeled a "blamer": whatever distressed him had to be someone else's fault.

"I told you the new car was a mistake," Mr. de

Haven grumbled at his wife. "After she cracked up the Buick, I was against buying her another car."

Mrs. de Haven reacted shrilly to what she interpreted as an accusation. "All right, it's *my* fault! How was Bethie going to get to her classes without transportation? She wouldn't have. . . ."

"She'd have stayed at home," Mr. de Haven accused. "This wouldn't have happened."

Beth's mother extracted a lace-trimmed handkerchief from her monstrous alligator bag and began sniffing. "My poor little girl! Oh, Clark, did you see all those bandages? Her face. . . ."

"Never could stop her from driving like a maniac." Mr. de Haven cursed quietly. "I knew it was coming. I was all set to have dinner with Newton. Close the deal and fly home. When they paged me from the hotel desk, I could have told you right then, it's Beth. Some other damned problem with Beth."

Janet fidgeted on the edge of a plastic settee, understanding, now, her beautiful boarder's alienation from these people. They had been permitted a brief visit to Beth's room. Since that time the tension between them had been rising, with Janet growing increasingly uncomfortable at being forced to eavesdrop on their personal bickering. It wouldn't have required a degree in psychology to recognize guilt at the root of their hostilities. Perhaps it would be better to await word from Lloyd elsewhere, Janet decided.

She was considering excusing herself and going to one of the staff lounges, when the de Haven's conversation took a significant turn. Suddenly, instead of blaming each other or Beth for the tragedy, they were . . . it was inconceivable! . . . they were pinning the responsibility on Beth's doctor.

"I *know* Beth hasn't been driving fast anymore," Mrs. de Haven was saying. "That last letter we had, Clark, remember? When she needed more money because her room and board fee had been increased?"

Janet looked up sharply. There had been no increase in the modest fee Beth had been paying for lodging. What . . . ?

"Beth positively assured me that she had finally learned her lesson and was driving *very* cautiously." Mrs. de Haven had stopped her pacing and had seated herself next to her husband, directly opposite Janet's settee. "Now, you *know* she wouldn't have crashed her car into a tree unless she . . . well, we *know* she didn't drink." The eyes that were so reminiscent of Beth's, yet so unlike them, narrowed in suspicion. "She *did* write that her new doctor was giving her medication to ease her headaches. She asked for money to cover the prescription costs, remember?"

"Eighty-five dollars," Mr. de Haven recalled grudgingly. "Some medicine."

"Don't you see, darling? Beth was probably under the influence of some drug. And I'd be willing to bet nobody warned her about possible side effects."

The de Havens had reached a perfect accord. "I don't like that doctor's looks," Beth's father said. "The way they're grinding out these half-baked young medics these days. What's his name? Lerner? Turner? Doesn't look old enough to be dry behind the ears. We never authorized him to give Bethie any damned drugs." While Janet sat, openmouthed with shock, Mr. de Haven sprang to his feet like a man with an urgent mission. "They won't tell us the truth here. They cover up for each other — regular protective fraternity."

"Where are you going, Clark?" his wife asked.

"I'm going to phone Peterson," he said.

"Darling, he doesn't practice here. Getting our own doctor from New York won't. . . ."

"Beth's in there dying!" Mr. de Haven roared. "Do you want her in the hands of some young punk who probably caused her accident in the first place? I want tests made! No quack's going to get away with anything if *I* can help it!"

"Mr. de Haven?" Janet was on her feet, but her fingertips touched the settee's arm for support, her legs trembling under her. The paunchy man scowled at her over his glasses. Mrs. de Haven pinned her under an imperious gaze. "Dr. Turner is a highly respected physician. He hasn't left your daughter's side since she was admitted this afternoon, and he's called in every specialist available — done everything he can to help Beth."

Janet had never seen a more vindictive expression on a man's face. "I should think he *would* try to keep Beth alive," Mr. de Haven sneered. "If he's been dosing her with drugs, he just might find himself facing a . . . manslaughter charge if our little girl doesn't pull through."

Mrs. de Haven released a shrill howl. "Don't say that! Oh, Clark, she can't die! My lovely doll-baby. . . ."

Janet ignored the theatrical sobbing that followed. "I know you're terribly upset, Mr. de Haven, but I don't think you want to make a serious charge like that. I know Dr. Turner. I'm a nurse here at the hospital, and I know he was very concerned about Beth. He. . . ."

Mr. de Haven turned away from Janet as though she were beneath his contempt. Addressing his wife, who had not been able to maintain her role as the anguished mother, he murmured, "I told you these people stick together, Lucille. She's a nurse. Charging us three-fifty a month to keep Beth, turns the poor kid over to some incompetent who's probably her boyfriend, and now we're supposed to believe Beth deliberately aimed her car at a tree. A beautiful nineteen-year-old girl . . . popular . . . all the spending money she could want. Next thing you know they'll be telling us Beth tried to commit suicide!" Mr. de Haven spun around and marched toward the public phone booth near the elevators, his face red with a frustrated need for vengeance.

Beth had lied to her parents, then, about the cost of her room and board. What had she done with the nearly two hundred dollars extra that the de Havens sent for that purpose? Drugs? It seemed inconceivable.

Maybe she DID want to kill herself, Janet thought dumbly. *You made her life a hell on earth. Maybe she was nothing but a source of trouble to you, but she knew you didn't love her. You don't even know how to love her now!*

The words couldn't be expressed, of course. And the thought was made even more painful by Janet's agonized memory: *I failed her, too! Beth was sick and confused. She needed someone to love and understand her — even defied me to give her the affection she didn't get at home. And I ordered her out of my house! I'm more to blame than these despicable people!*

Too depressed to wait any longer in the company of Beth's parents, Janet made her way to a usually unoccupied cluster of chairs at the end of the corridor. Approaching, she saw that the dejected figure seated there, his head in his hands, was Denny Reese.

He nodded his acknowledgment as Janet sat down beside him, but he was quiet. Engaging Denny in conversation would have forced him to raise his head — and no grown man wanted to be seen crying.

They sat in silence until Lloyd Turner came out of Beth's room, gravely advising them that there was little point in waiting; Beth was unconscious. He expected no further changes.

"*Further* changes?" Janet grasped at the straw of hope.

"She regained consciousness for a few seconds," Lloyd said somberly. He looked exhausted, and Janet had never seen a doctor more emotionally affected by a patient's battle to survive. "Just for a few seconds," Lloyd repeated wearily. "Unbelievable. She recognized me and she . . . smiled."

Denny was drinking the words in hungrily. "If she did that . . . she's going to make it, isn't she, Doctor? If she was able to. . . ."

Lloyd's grimly set features promised nothing. "She looked directly at me, and she said, 'You lose, Doc. My head *still* hurts'." Lloyd's eyes met Janet's for a searching instant. "That's Beth," his expression said. "Beautiful little female 'Pagliacci.' She's going to die, but you know she's going to leave you with a flip remark."

It was strange, Janet thought, how two people who had once loved each other could still communicate the most subtle message without the use of words. Lloyd was still fighting, but when you knew him as well as Janet knew him, you read his inner thoughts; Beth was going to be spared a life of disfigurement and added pain. *"You lose, Doc."* In one fleeting moment of consciousness, she had known. And, typically, she had brushed off the final tragedy of her life with a wisecrack.

Lloyd reached out to touch Denny's shoulder with his hand, a gesture that was more consoling than reassuring. "Her mother and dad will want to hear from me," he said.

Janet's misery, as her eyes followed Lloyd's weary walk toward the place where the de Havens waited for him, was not for Beth alone. She wanted to walk beside him, to stand between him and the two people who had projected their neglect upon his shoulders, to assure him that she believed in him, not only as a doctor, but also as a man.

Lloyd preferred to walk alone; he was no longer a part of her life. After a long while, Janet said, "We aren't helping Beth by staying here. Dr. Turner's right. If we get some rest. . . ."

"I'll come back in the morning." Denny got up obediently and accompanied Janet to the elevator. The last thing Janet heard before the elevator doors separated her from the trio in the waiting room was Mr. de Haven's threatening voice: ". . . prove you had Beth on drugs, I'll sue you for malpractice, and, by God, I'll see that you lose your license to practice!"

ELEVEN

By noon on Tuesday, Janet admitted to her head nurse that perhaps it had been a mistake to come to work. "It's not fair to my patients," she sighed as she stepped into the nurses' station to sign out for lunch. "I've got Beth de Haven on my mind. I have to keep reminding myself that these other people are sick, too."

Head Nurse Ruth Garland understood. A fiftyish woman, whose Dutch-boy haircut and placid face made her appear younger, she was nevertheless one of the more experienced R.N.'s who could truthfully say that they had "seen it all." "I think everyone in the hospital feels the same way, Janet," she said. "I've probably called the I.C.U. desk a dozen times this morning, and I even walked over there during my break."

Janet didn't have to ask for a report. During her own coffee break she had talked to one of the Specials who kept a constant vigil in Beth's room. Except for the brief moment when Beth had recognized and spoken to Lloyd Turner, she had not regained consciousness.

"I can't remember seeing a medical team work as hard as they've been working to keep that girl alive," Mrs. Garland said. "I can't imagine what the de Havens hope to gain by taking Dr. Turner off the case."

Janet had half-expected this development, yet the news came as a shock. "They didn't!"

Mrs. Garland made a disparaging gesture. "They tried to get their family doctor to come out here, but he wasn't available. So now Dr. Harrison's in charge, I understand."

Turning responsibility for the patient over to the hospital's Chief of Staff meant that Beth was, technically, a house patient. Dismissing an attending physician without calling in another private doctor was almost unheard of. Certainly the move reflected upon Lloyd's capability.

"When people get frantic, they do some strange things," Mrs. Garland concluded. If she knew that the de Havens blamed Lloyd Turner for their daughter's accident, the head nurse discreetly pretended ignorance. But, remembering that Janet had been engaged to the doctor, she added, "Dr. Turner seems terribly depressed. I've been debating whether it'll do more harm than good to tell him I'm. . . ." Mrs. Garland hesitated, probably searching for a way of conveying her sympathy without breaking any rules of ethics. "You don't know whether he'd like it better if you pretended you hadn't heard the rumors at all, or if . . . well, I'd like to tell him *I* know he did everything possible for the little de Haven girl. God knows there isn't a young doctor I respect more. And you'd never get *me* to believe he prescribed drugs without warning a patient about their side effects."

The de Havens' accusation was common knowledge, then. And perhaps Mrs. Garland was using this means to tell Janet that Lloyd Turner could use some moral support. Not that anyone in the hospital would believe the ugly inferences made by two people who knew nothing at all about medical procedures, but what doctor wouldn't be depressed under the circumstances?

Especially a doctor who felt that he had failed in getting his patient under proper care?

"I'll talk to Dr. Turner when I get a chance," Janet promised.

Her intuition was right. "I was hoping you'd say that," the head nurse told her. "I don't know anything about your personal differences with him, dear, but I *do* know he'd appreciate a . . . vote of confidence."

Janet spoke to another doctor first, and the comments he added made it all the more imperative that Lloyd be given moral support. During lunch in the staff dining room, Rick Wexton was untypically solemn when Janet brought up the subject of the de Havens.

"You can attribute part of their attitude to the emotional state they're in," Rick conceded. "Assuming that their daughter survives . . . and that's an overly optimistic assumption . . . she's going to face years of plastic surgery, and even then, she isn't ever going to be the girl they knew. With the shock of disfigurement you get inevitable personality changes. You can understand where Beth's parents wouldn't be completely rational at this time." Rick stirred his coffee, quietly thoughtful for a moment. Then he said, "I'll grant you that there's a vindictive streak in both those people. On the other hand, they may have some grounds for their opinions."

Janet looked up from the tasteless dessert with which she had been toying. She sounded and felt defensive as she asked, "What does that mean?"

"In the strictest confidence, of course. . . ."

"Yes?"

"The patient *was* under the influence of barbiturates," Rick said. "She had a regular arsenal of drugs in her handbag, including codeine. She couldn't have gotten barbiturates or codeine without a prescription. She hadn't consulted any other doctor in the area. And when I saw her at your house, there wasn't any doubt that she was high on something."

Janet's spoon trembled in her hand. "What does that mean, Rick?"

He released a whooshing breath of air. "It means that I'd have to testify to that fact if an investigation comes up. Understand, the girl *could* have been driving against Turner's orders. We can't control a patient's actions once they leave the office. The problem is. . . ."

"Yes?"

"Beth was in possession of an excess of medication, and Turner knew she was racing around town in a car. Furthermore, she's a minor . . . and a strong-willed, very independent kid, at that. I can't even imagine a pharmacist not questioning the quantity of drugs the police found in her car. And I certainly can't imagine an M.D. prescribing all those goodies. Tranquilizers, pep pills, analgesics, enough barbiturates to stock a small clinic." Rick shook his head. "And *codeine*. Hand all that to an irresponsible minor who's already got a long string of traffic accidents behind her! It amounts to . . . in this case, everything the de Havens are saying."

"I don't believe Lloyd's responsible," Janet argued. "He told me she walked out of his office before he was able to do anything for her!"

"Pharmacists keep records," Rick said in a bland tone. "It's being checked."

"Yes, and I'm positive Lloyd didn't write prescriptions for. . . ."

"It's a sickening thought," Rick said. "But he could have handed the stuff over the desk. Pharmaceutical house samples. I've done it, on occasion. Save the patient some money." Rick thought about the statement and all its implications for a few seconds. "It's just a thought," he said. "Strictly between us. I wouldn't say it to anyone else."

"I wish you hadn't said it at all." Janet set her teaspoon down, her stomach churning.

Rick shrugged off the tension of the moment. "We can sit here and conjecture all day, honey. Point is, it's a bad scene and there's nothing we can do about it. If there's been professional negligence, it'll come to light under investigation."

"Then . . . there *is* an investigation."

"Don't you think the circumstances call for one?"

Rick's question haunted Janet for the rest of the day. Lloyd was not infallible. He was human. Concerned about Beth's "excruciating" headaches, what if he had prescribed codeine — even forbidden her to drive her car? He could be regretting his decision now, torn up by its tragic result, under pressure from the Chief of Staff and other authorities. Mrs. Garland had guessed correctly; right or wrong, Lloyd needed his friends now more than ever before. And Janet had been more than a friend. The season's first snowfall that morning had brought remembrances of the approaching Christmastime. They had planned to be married during the holidays. . . .

Janet was unable to find Lloyd alone until seven, when he came into the hospital for his evening rounds. She had phoned Aunt Cammie, reporting on the unencouraging visit to Beth's room and saying that she would not be home for dinner. Then she had killed part of the waiting time in the staff dining room forcing down another uninspired meal, and another half hour trying to ease the qualms of another regular visitor to the Intensive Care Unit, Denny Reese. They were both too depressed to exchange anything but meaningless platitudes. It was a relief to get away from the miserable young man and to learn that Dr. Turner had seen the last of his patients and was on his way out of the hospital.

Janet stopped him in one of the third-floor corridors, wondering, after they had exchanged stiff greetings, what she could say next. Come right out and remind him that the whole staff was talking about his problem? Offer an awkward, uninvited assurance that he was not the monster Beth's parents had painted him to be?

There was a long, uncomfortable silence before Janet managed to stammer, "I just . . . I'd like you to know that I don't believe . . . that I'm sure you did all you could for Beth."

"I don't happen to agree," Lloyd said. His face remained impassive, but he avoided her eyes. "I wasn't able to do anything at all for her — not even to complete my diagnosis."

Janet felt her face smarting under the cold rebuff. "I meant . . . no matter what anyone says, I know that you . . . you didn't. . . ."

"If you're trying to assure me that I'm a responsible physician," Lloyd said curtly, "it isn't necessary, thanks. My conscience is quite clear on that score. Exactly as clear as it was when you accused me of a *personal* involvement with Beth."

Lloyd had been hurt, and he was striking back. It was understandable, but understanding didn't make this encounter less painful. Janet's fingernails dug into her palms. "I was only. . . ."

"Thank you," Lloyd said. He might have been addressing a total stranger who had patronized him. "It's good to know that you don't think I dismissed a patient with a bucketful of conflicting drugs. Considering that you had so little faith in me personally, it's wonderful to hear that you don't think I'm an unethical pill pusher."

Lloyd's tone cut through her like a scalpel. Janet could think of nothing else to say, nothing that wouldn't have sounded condescending. Lloyd seemed eager to be on his way. She apologized for delaying him, swallowed hard, and stepped aside to let him pass.

The meeting would have been traumatic enough for Janet if Lloyd hadn't taken several steps, then turned around to say, "Incidentally, the bank okayed my loan this morning. You should be getting your check soon for the ten thousand, plus interest. I'm afraid I don't know how to thank you."

"I don't want the money," Janet cried. "Why should you pay a high interest rate when I don't need. . . ."

"*I* needed to do it this way," Lloyd said. "I'm sorry I couldn't have repaid you sooner."

He was saying, of course, that he wished he had never accepted the loan. Costly as it might be, borrowing the money from an impersonal bank freed him completely. It was what he wanted.

"If that's what you want. . . ."

Janet's resentful sentence was cut off by a polite "good night" from Lloyd. He was on his way to the elevators before Janet could reply, and, once again, it was only her resentment of his stubborn pride that quieted the other emotions Lloyd had evoked. Anger was still a good antidote for misery.

TWELVE

Janet's defenses lasted only until she stepped into her own living room. One glance at Aunt Cammie's red-rimmed eyes, and she was in tears herself.

They sat on opposite sides of the room, Janet looking out the window, saying nothing. The street light threw shadows of the leafless elm trees across the snow-covered front yard — bleak, twisted branch shapes woven into a bizarre pattern. Cammie had let the flames die down in the fireplace, yet the room felt oppressively warm.

They had been quiet for so long that Cammie's voice broke the silence with a startling effect. "I had to do something with my hands tonight," she said. "With you out of the house, I wanted something to do . . . anything to get my mind off of. . . ." Cammie's plump wrist swiped at her eyes. "You know."

Janet made a studied effort to smile. "So what did you do? Got something to show me?"

Cammie shook her head. "I remembered Beth showing me a picture in one of the women's magazines . . . these ornate little hand-mirrors with papier-mâché frames, all painted in bright poster colors and then sprayed with clear lacquer. I told her I could pick up a cheap mirror and do a copy of the one she liked — make it for a fraction of what they get in the gift shops." Huge tears had started rolling down Cammie's cheeks, but she ignored them now. "Beth liked one of the patterns best of all. It was quite a challenge. All sorts of crazy little birds and flowers, but I'm pretty good at flowers, and I thought I could trace the birds. Anyway, tonight I thought . . . oh, Jan, what was wrong with me? I thought I'd make it as a present for Beth. Surprise her, when she's feeling better. I kept thinking of how she called the pattern 'campy' and 'groovy' and all those other words she'd use when she liked something. A pie I'd made, or. . . ."

Janet knew what was coming. She tried to divert Cammie's mind from the poignant error in judgment. "Beth was always a real fan of yours, wasn't she?"

Cammie tried to answer, but she found it impossible to express herself in words. *Why haven't I realized,* Janet thought, *how much Cammie needed the kind of appreciation she got from Beth? I've always taken her for granted. Token compliments when she turned out some useless little artsy-craftsy thing, but never the lavish enthusiasm Beth poured out. As though I couldn't see that Cammie's china-paint flowers and her Popsicle stick wren houses . . . all the artless things she makes with her hands are beautiful in her eyes. They're all she has in her life except mundane jobs.*

Another thought swelled into Janet's mind:

Beth had excellent taste. She couldn't have been impressed by Cammie's plastic-fiber geraniums, yet she held them up in her hand, admiring them from every angle, rained praise on Cammie's "astounding artistic ability," and asked if she could have a few for the dressing table in her room. *Beth had understood a lonely, loveless woman's need, and she had cared!* No wonder Cammie, who had been stoic and dry-eyed at her own brother's funeral, was crying openly now.

"What was the matter with me? A *mirror!* I was going to make a fancy-framed *mirror* for that poor little thing. Oh, Lord, Janet, I almost think it would be better if . . . if she could just stay asleep and never have to look at that horror. . . ."

"You don't mean that," Janet said gently. On impulse, she got up, crossed the room, and leaned down to plant a kiss on Cammie's temple. She spared her aunt knowledge of the other tragedies in Beth de Haven's life: her desperate search for escape through drugs and parents who seemed more concerned with revenge than seeing their only child recover.

There was one other member of Cammie's fan club. He, too, had praised her creative efforts, and he had thoughtfully provided her with such vital craft supplies as tongue depressors and glue. Considerately, Janet said nothing about the problems facing Lloyd Turner.

It was Cammie who mentioned her favorite doctor. "I shouldn't have said that. No, I'm going to go right on praying for Beth. I know Dr.

Turner's not giving up."

"Of course he isn't," Janet replied. She had to hurry out of the room as she said it. Cammie's perceptive eyes would have seen the truth written on Janet's face, and it would have broken her heart to know that Beth was no longer under Dr. Turner's care.

THIRTEEN

Janet came home from the hospital two days later with the same discouraging news that she had been reporting to her aunt since the accident. Beth remained locked in a deathlike coma. She was being fed intravenously, and her respiration would have ceased without the use of oxygen. Beth's failing pulse and temperature and her lack of response to medication depressed whatever hope the staff had held for her recovery.

"There's got to be *something* Dr. Turner can do!" Cammie said. She was still unaware of Lloyd's dismissal.

"It's puzzling," Janet told her. "If there were bone fragments in the brain or pressure from a bone the doctors might remedy the condition surgically. But it's nothing like that. It's as though. . . ."

"As though Beth had just decided that she doesn't want to live anymore?" Cammie asked.

Janet nodded.

"Poor Dr. Turner." Cammie gestured toward the stairway. "By the way, you got a letter from him today. It's up on your dresser."

"I've been expecting it." Janet started toward the steps. Then, seeing the hopeful curiosity on her aunt's face, she said, "It's probably the check. He's returning the money I loaned him."

"I see." Cammie's expression had called for a letter of reconciliation and she was not successful in hiding her disappointment.

Janet shared the reaction when she opened the envelope addressed in Lloyd's familiar hand. She had half hoped for a longer note than the simple "Thank you" Lloyd had signed and enclosed. Janet slipped the check into a dresser drawer, reminding herself that it didn't matter. Lloyd was someone who belonged to the past. Rick Wexton was coming by for her at eight; he had said he was determined to take her out and shake her out of her depression. Janet opened her closet door to select a dress, trying hard to concentrate on the future.

Janet was laying out the clothes she would wear that evening when Phyllis passed by the open bedroom door. She had already asked about Beth. Now, pausing in the open doorway she said, "Are you going back to the hospital, Janet?"

"No. Why?"

Phyllis edged into the room, waiting for an invitation before crossing the threshold. When Janet had motioned for her to come in, Phyllis positioned herself awkwardly near a high chest. "I just wondered. I thought . . . you might be . . . going to talk to Dr. Turner. Maybe . . . about Beth, or something."

Janet frowned. "I don't understand."

Phyllis looked embarrassed. "Well . . . I knew you got a letter from Dr. Turner, and . . . naturally, I'm interested. If there's any news about Beth, I. . . ."

"If Dr. Turner had information about Beth's condition, I'm sure he wouldn't put it into a letter." Janet was surprised by the irritation in her tone. Phyllis was not terribly bright, and the slightest criticism would bring tears to her eyes. More gently, Janet explained, "It wasn't a real letter, anyway. Just a . . . financial matter."

Phyllis seemed oddly relieved. "Oh." She shifted from one foot to the other, making Janet wonder if this self-conscious creature could ever acquire the poise expected of a nurse. "I noticed you were getting ready to go out, so I. . . ." Phyllis blushed. "You ought to tell me to mind my own business."

"Not at all," Janet assured her. "I'm going out with Dr. Wexton. A play at the college."

Phyllis rarely smiled, but now she beamed with pleasure. "That's wonderful. Dr. Wexton's *so* nice, and he's *so* good-looking. You're so much better off going out with him."

Janet controlled a sudden annoyance, curious to know what Phyllis had on her mind; obviously this was not just idle chatter. "Do you think so?" Janet encouraged.

"Oh, yes. Dr. Wexton's pretty well off, from the way he dresses and from that car he drives. And he's got an awfully good reputation, I hear." Phyllis hesitated, as though she were testing the reception of her words.

"He's a highly respected internist," Janet agreed. The girl was getting at something. But what?

"If you were married to someone like that, you wouldn't have to worry about whether he was interested in you, or if he just needed money to get started on. I don't want to say anything bad about Dr. Turner . . . he's been just wonderful to me . . . but . . . right now, you're better off not being mixed up in all this trouble he's having."

"Trouble?" It was getting more difficult for Janet to stay calm.

"You know. The things you hear. I heard him talking to someone on the phone yesterday while I was working in the office, and . . . it sounded like he was very upset. After all, everybody knows Beth was taking some kind of pills. She kept them hidden under her sweaters in the second drawer."

"Really?"

Phyllis turned a deep shade of scarlet. "Don't think I snooped. I . . . saw her hiding a bottle of pills when I came into her room once."

Janet had fixed the girl with a penetrating stare. "You can't be sure it wasn't just aspirin."

"People don't hide aspirin," Phyllis said. "And that business of her driving the car. I told you I was scared to death those times she drove me home from Dr. Turner's office. He must have seen the way Beth roared off. She drove like a maniac. Everybody knew that."

"What are you trying to say, Phyllis?"

Phyllis twisted her knuckles, her eyes evasive. "Nothing. Just that . . . it's nice that you aren't mixed up in any of this trouble. I wouldn't repeat any of this to anyone except you . . . I mean, about Dr. Turner. Anybody can make a mistake. I still think he's . . . a wonderful doctor."

"I still think so, too," Janet said pointedly. "And I don't think we want to discuss this any further. Do you?"

"No. No, it's all too depressing," Phyllis said. "That's why I'm so glad you're getting to go out and enjoy yourself, instead of having more worries on your mind. Dr. Wexton's just crazy about you. I can tell." Phyllis turned, virtually skipping out of the bedroom. "Don't let me hold you up. I know you want to look nice tonight, and I'm just so happy for you . . . you can't imagine!"

Janet attributed the burst of animation to emotional instability. Phyllis, having no admirers of her own, evidently lived vicariously, and Janet's budding romance with a "well-off, good-looking" doctor was exciting to her. Perhaps the girl's loneliness accounted for her curiosity about other people's mail and other people's actions. She would have to be told to avoid gossip, especially discussions of her employer. But this confidential talk with one of the few people who took time to listen to her was excusable. Lonely, Janet decided. She regretted her earlier irritation with Phyllis, remembering the mistake she had made in rejecting Beth.

Dressing for her theatre date with Rick later, Janet made a mental note to talk to her aunt about Phyllis. Cammie barely spoke to the girl, and heaven knew Phyllis had enough personality problems without being made to feel guilty about Beth's departure. Cammie had led a loveless life; certainly she could be made to understand.

FOURTEEN

"It's not that it wasn't a good play," Janet said. "If I didn't seem to be enjoying it, it's only because I . . . I guess I have other things on my mind."

She had asked Rick Wexton to have coffee at her home after the performance, and though he usually promoted a favorite chic restaurant for after-theatre snacks, tonight, surprisingly, he had accepted Janet's invitation. While Janet prepared the coffee, Rick had stirred up the glowing embers in the fireplace, adding a log which blazed brightly now, providing welcome warmth as well as the room's only light. (Rick had apparently turned off the lamps while Janet was in the kitchen.)

Seated beside Rick on a massive, chintz-covered sofa, Janet stared at the sputtering flames. "I really owe you an apology, Rick. I haven't been the best company lately."

"I suppose I can understand that," Rick said. "From your point of view, that is. You're depressed about the de Haven girl, and it's a sorry situation, true. You're going to have to start divorcing yourself from other people's problems, though. Otherwise you're going to spend your life being miserable over the way someone else chose to mess up his or her own life."

Rick reached over to close his hand over Janet's. "Honey, a few months back this girl was a total stranger to you. I'll grant you, it's a tragic case, and you're bound to feel a certain amount of empathy with someone who's lived in your home. Possibly even a shade of responsibility for what happened. Although, I was here when you asked the girl to leave, and you were certainly justified. She created a disturbance and you did the only thing you could do."

Janet felt Rick's fingers tighten their grip. He was making sense, she knew — yet how meaningless the words sounded! It was impossible to tell him that there was another reason for her somber mood tonight. Besides, she had promised herself not to think about Lloyd. . . .

"I'd like to see you happy, Janet," Rick was saying. "The only way to be happy is to avoid getting involved, especially in situations you can't change. Beth was heading for a crack-up of one kind or another from the day she was born. Did you think you could undo what people like the de Havens can do to an only child? And that other albatross you've got around your neck! What's her name, Phoebe?"

"Phyllis."

"Okay, Phyllis. There's a born loser if I ever met one. You could get so wrapped up in trying to get acceptance for *her* that you'd become a drag yourself."

It was a startling thought. How many times,

Janet wondered, have I bored Rick with tales about Phyllis Straley's petty problems? Maybe Lloyd was tired of the subject, too. He had found her obsequious manner and whining voice tiresome around his office. "You're probably right," Janet admitted.

"I know I'm right, darling." Rick released Janet's hand and put his arms around her. "Sweetheart, you've got to stop taking on problems you can't solve. You only get hurt. Loaning people money usually makes them resent you; try to straighten them out and you get accused of meddling."

"I haven't had any financial dealings with Phyllis," Janet said testily. She had never told Rick about the loan to Lloyd Turner; at the time, it hadn't been a loan at all, but a sharing with the man she was to marry.

"I just used that as an example of a good way to burden yourself and alienate people," Rick said.

If he knew more than Janet wanted him to know, at least his explanation sounded plausible. Janet chose to believe him. Besides, there was no more time for analyzing sensitive statements. Rick was murmuring, "I love you, Janet. I don't want you to fall into the same trap I fell into once. Think about your own happiness. You don't know how much I want to make you happy." He kissed her firmly, and Janet realized how tired she was of propping up other people, when her own being cried out for love, for this sort of male strength and solid judgment to lean on. Beth, Cammie, Phyllis, Lloyd . . . they weren't children. She had not made their decisions for them. How long could she go on wearing herself sick with worry over problems she had not created?

Janet let herself be held tightly, responding to the kisses of a man who asked nothing of her. Nothing except, now, her love.

"I'd like to get you out of this archaic house. You're young and you're living in a museum. You should be surrounded by color, new things, music. That's the kind of setting I've made for myself at my apartment. All it lacks is you."

Rick interrupted his persuasive lecture to kiss Janet again. "Please, darling. I want to make a new kind of life for you. You're too beautiful, too sharp to be living like a . . . housemother in a dormitory for neurotics."

"I couldn't. . . ."

"You can't leave this confining place? Start living? You've *got* to, Janet."

Confused, knowing that the arguments were valid, Janet still found it difficult to project herself into the future Rick was proposing.

Rick must have sensed her thoughts, because he said, "I'm not asking for an immediate decision, dear. You're disturbed about the de Haven girl, and I haven't given you time to think." His arms tightened around Janet, and there was no mistaking Rick's sincerity as he whispered, "If it means anything to you, darling, I need you more than anyone else needs you. I love you . . . I want you. Please don't disappoint me, Janet. I want you where I can reach out and take you into my arms . . . for the rest of our lives."

Later, in the quiet darkness of her room, Janet projected herself forward, picturing herself as the wife of a handsome, successful physician, one who, unlike Lloyd Turner, left his work behind him and knew what a woman wants to hear when she's alone with a man. Rick Wexton was fun. He was thoughtful, he was romantic, he was highly respected by his colleagues, and he knew how to enjoy life. There were few unmarried nurses at the hospital who didn't envy Janet because he had singled her out for attention.

And what was the alternative? More icy encounters with Lloyd? Wasting a lifetime hoping that a man who had once planned to marry her would change his mind and want her again? Aunt Cammie had made a similar mistake. She had fallen in love with a man who barely knew she existed, ignoring all others until it was too late. I don't want to find myself alone when I'm Cammie's age, Janet thought. I want a husband, a home of my own, children — not a lot of silly hobbies to fill my time and to ward off loneliness.

It was late at night — far too late to be lying in bed weighing decisions, when you knew the alarm would ring at six. Beth, Lloyd Turner, the beloved old house, Rick — thoughts whirled through Janet's mind, fragmented, changing as swiftly as the colors and patterns of a kaleidoscope. Was she in love with Rick? She enjoyed his company, and she felt awakened by his kisses; was it necessary to thrill to the sound of a man's voice, or find her heart beating faster, the way she had once reacted when Lloyd walked into a room?

Love seemed indefinable, and whenever Janet visualized herself as Mrs. Richard Wexton, the specters of Beth de Haven and Lloyd returned to intrude upon the perfect picture.

Exhausted by indecision, Janet closed her eyes. Her last thought before drifting off into sleep would have been jarring, except that it seemed inconceivable that Rick had been proposing anything but marriage. He hadn't actually used the word. But he had assumed it, of course. "For the rest of my life," he had said. There was no doubt about it: He wanted Janet to be his wife.

FIFTEEN

It could have been considerably more humiliating, Janet reflected later. She could have taken
one of the other nurses into her confidence, and
the story of Dr. Wexton's "marriage proposal"
would have spread through the wards like wild
flowers. As it was, she was spared not only the
embarrassment of having made a fool of herself
before other members of the hospital staff, but
Rick was never given the opportunity to call her
naïve.

Ironically, it was Lloyd Turner who opened
Janet's eyes. Janet was carrying a medicine tray
out of a room occupied by one of Lloyd's patients when the doctor arrived on his morning
rounds. Almost colliding with him outside the
door, Janet mumbled a greeting and said that the
patient's Special was anxious to see the doctor.

"Yes, she phoned me at the office," Lloyd ac-
knowledged. "No problem, except convincing
Mr. Nichols that he's far from ready to be released."

"That may take some doing." Janet smiled,
wondering, meanwhile, why the tray shook in
her hands. "He's been ordering me to pack his
suitcase all morning. Says he's going home
today, and no back talk from any of us."

"I suppose he's taking all the plumbing we've got in him, too." Lloyd shook his head, familiar with the eccentricities of his elderly patient. "Might have to glue old Nichols to the bed if we don't want him bolting out through the window. If you see him tying sheets together, yell for help."

"He does all the yelling," Janet said. "Right now, he's yelling for you."

"I'll see what I can do to detain our boy. At least until we can remove his stitches."

Lloyd reached for the doorknob, ending the facetious chatter. It had been a long time since they had exchanged this sort of relaxed small talk, and Janet wished that it could have gone on. She started toward the nurses' station, then turned as Lloyd called her name.

"Yes, Doctor?"

Lloyd was still standing in the corridor. "I wondered if you'd gotten the check. I'm sorry it took so long, but. . . ."

"You didn't have to. . . ."

"I had to," he said flatly.

"All right, but . . . paying bank interest when I don't really need the money. . . ."

"New friends, new expenses," Lloyd said. There was an expression of bemused disgust on his face. "My replacement might be able to use a few bucks toward the support of his wife and three kids."

Janet could only gape at him.

"He isn't divorced yet, so it can't be called alimony." Lloyd shrugged. "Make a contribution toward temporary child support. Maybe your boyfriend won't have to go to such pains to avoid personal calls from New York."

Janet made an attempt to sound indignant, but her voice quavered. "I hope you know what you're talking about."

"Oh, I *do*," Lloyd said with exaggerated politeness. "And I'm a little surprised that you don't. Especially since everyone else seems to know Dr. Wexton came here to run away from personal responsibilities. His wife's having a devil of a time trying to reach him." Lloyd faked a gentlemanly bowing gesture. "As any of our switchboard operators may, or may not, have told you."

Burning with shame, Janet stammered, "You . . . you know I wouldn't go out with a man if I . . . if I knew he was. . . ."

"I'd better get in here and have it out with Superman," Lloyd said. He had opened the door and was greeting old Mr. Nichols effusively from the doorway before Janet could recover from her shock and move on down the corridor.

Shock. Revulsion. Anger. During her walk toward the charge desk, Janet examined her reactions as objectively as if she were viewing someone else's emotions under a microscope. *Embarrassment. Annoyance with Lloyd's smug manner. Self-disgust for having been such a poor judge of character.* These were all included in a rush of intense feeling, but there was no pain. Oddly, there was even a vague sensation of relief.

Yet last night Janet had been giving serious consideration to a marriage proposal that had, in reality, been only a common proposition. Recalling Rick Wexton's words, now, and his suave, guarded approach, Janet tore into the nurses' station in a silent fury that was aimed less at the man who had caused her humiliation than at the man who had faced her with the truth. Her reason was all too apparent; she had never loved Rick Wexton. He wasn't important. Being cheapened in Lloyd Turner's eyes was another matter. She had loved him once. Now, in the midst of her blazing anger with him, Janet knew that she would always love him.

Mrs. Garland was away from her desk, but the absence of the head nurse still didn't allow for the kind of release Janet needed; the nurses' station was hardly the place to slam down whatever objects came to hand. Besides, the telephone was ringing, barely heard over the speakers, over which Dr. Harrison was being paged.

Janet took a deep breath, released it, and picked up the telephone receiver. "Yes?"

A familiar female voice asked, "Mrs. Garland?"

"Mrs. Garland isn't here. May I help you?"

"Miss Leland?" Janet identified the caller as Adeline Colby, head nurse in charge of the Intensive Care Unit. "I really wanted to reach *you*. I'm afraid we . . . have bad news."

Janet froze. "Beth," she whispered.

"I'm sorry, Miss Leland. The Special just

came to the station, asking us to page Dr. Harrison. He had asked to be called personally to certify. . . ."

It was senseless. Janet had visited Beth's room before reporting for duty only a few hours earlier, and, although Beth had not stirred in her deep coma — her folded hands waxen and motionless — imminent death had seemed, somehow, unthinkable.

"Miss Leland . . . are you there?"

Janet was too dazed to reply. After a long, breathless silence, the question was repeated, and she managed to say, "Thank you for . . . letting me know." Then she dropped the receiver into its cradle, lowered her head to the desk, and let the tears come.

The sound of footsteps brought Janet to her feet. This was still a hospital; the charge desk was no place for a display of personal grief. Blotting her eyes with a folded Kleenex, she turned her back on whoever was approaching and made a pretense of busying herself with a medications chart at the back desk.

"Janet?" The sympathetic voice belonged to Mrs. Garland. Janet turned to see that the head nurse was not alone. Rick Wexton was with her.

"I just heard," Mrs. Garland said quietly. "I know how you must feel, Janet. Would you like me to get a replacement for the rest of the day? We're shorthanded, but I think I can get Miss Bessler to. . . ."

Janet closed her eyes for a moment. "I'd rather

stay busy, Mrs. Garland. I'll be all right once I. . . ."

"I keep telling Janet that she's got to divorce herself emotionally from other people's problems." That was Dr. Wexton speaking. Janet heard the deep, carefully modulated, almost unctuous voice as though it were coming from another planet. "We're all sorry about losing a patient, but we have to regard these events as impersonally as possible. Dr. Turner made the mistake of taking a personal interest, and look what he's getting out of it — the patient's father downstairs screaming about a malpractice suit! The girl was mixed up before she came to your house, dear, and you mustn't let yourself get depressed by something you couldn't control. It's tragic, but you aren't responsible for. . . ."

He was going on and on. Saying something about picking Janet up at three, having a few drinks, and, later, going out to dinner at that new Italian place that had just opened up. On and on, consoling Janet by telling her indirectly that other people didn't matter; your own immediate pleasure was all that counted. "There's nothing you can do, girl. Let me help you try to forget the whole miserable. . . ."

"Don't talk to me!" Janet heard her own voice from another plane, too. Some stranger was shrilling at Rick Wexton, crying, "You don't care about anyone but yourself! If I listened to you, I'd become as callous and inhuman as you are! I don't want any part of your fancy dinners and

your cocktails and that sumptuous apartment you set up for yourself!"

"Janet. . . ." Mrs. Garland's gentle warning was ignored.

"You can talk to me about how to avoid responsibility! You're an expert! You don't even care if your own children are eating. You don't respect them, or me, or . . . you can't even have respect for yourself! You've lied to. . . ."

"Janet, I know you're upset, but we have patients on this floor!" Mrs. Garland issued the reminder in a firm tone. "Please settle your personal differences with Dr. Wexton somewhere else."

Janet's sobs were beyond control, but the head nurse's order had a sobering effect. Rick Wexton was staring at her with a mildly incredulous expression, as though it surprised him to see anyone give way to pure emotion. Janet had nothing more to say to him. *Beth de Haven was dead. Lloyd was being threatened by a malpractice suit.* The world seemed to be crumbling around her, and Janet's only instinct was to run.

"Go over to the lounge and try to compose yourself," Mrs. Garland was advising.

Janet didn't have to be told. She was hurrying out of the nurses' station, tears blurring her vision, unmindful of Rick Wexton's blasé dismissal of her:

"You'd think a trained R.N. would have better control of her emotions. Suppose we had hysteria everytime a patient died? This is intolerable in a hospital!"

Janet had been in the nurses' lounge for the better part of an hour before Ruth Garland came into the room. There was no one else present. The head nurse sat herself on the settee next to Janet, waited until she was sure there were no more sobs forthcoming, and then said, "I'm going to talk to you like a Dutch uncle, Janet. Whatever Dr. Wexton's shortcomings, he's not completely wrong. You've taken on too many problems. More than you can handle. And this terrible thing that's happened this morning was the breaking point. You know as well as I do that you don't lash out at a staff doctor in a voice that can be heard from one end of the corridor to the other."

"I shouldn't have done that," Janet admitted. "I was so . . ."

"I understand," Mrs. Garland said. "You wouldn't have made that scene if you hadn't been completely unnerved. That's why I'm going to recommend that you get away for a while."

Stunned, Janet turned to face the other woman. "It won't happen again, Mrs. Garland."

The head nurse patted Janet's hand. "I'm not dismissing you, child. I'm suggesting this for your own good. You've had a series of unpleasant experiences, and I foresee others."

"Other. . . ."

"Understand, this is confidential." Although

there was no one else in the lounge, Mrs. Garland peered around cautiously and lowered her tone. "With the possibility of a suit hanging over Dr. Turner's head, Administration is sure to conduct an inquiry of its own before a medical board. In a sense, it's . . . you might call it a protective measure. I'm sure Dr. Turner will be cleared. I'm *not* sure you ought to be here during the proceedings."

"I can't just run off! Lloyd . . . Dr. Turner will need witnesses. He. . . ."

"You can't contribute any valid medical testimony," Mrs. Garland said. "You weren't present during the patient's visits to Dr. Turner's office. I think you told me you weren't aware that Beth was taking any drugs. . . ."

"I wasn't. Phyllis Straley — the other student who's staying with us — she mentioned something about a cache of pills. But that wasn't until after the accident, and she didn't really know what or how much Beth was taking."

"Then you can't offer any testimony at all," Mrs. Garland concluded. "A medical board isn't going to be interested in your personal opinion of Dr. Turner. I don't see how you can be of any value to him by staying here, and you're going to have a complete breakdown if you don't get away. You need a good rest, a change of scene. Time to reorganize your thoughts. Take a vacation, Janet. Come back and start out fresh."

It was probably sound advice, Janet decided. Her nerves had been stretched taut since the breakup with Lloyd, and the quality of her service as a nurse had probably suffered. Now there would be the misery of telling Aunt Cammie that Beth was gone. There would be guilt-ridden whining by Phyllis and then the agony of a medical board hearing during which the unhappy experiences with Beth would be dredged to the surface. It would all be bearable if Lloyd wanted her at his side throughout the coming ordeal, but it was clear that she had not only lost his love, he had lost his respect for her.

"I took the liberty of sending for some literature that might interest you," Janet's superior was telling her. She snapped open her purse and extracted a thickly stuffed envelope, handing it to Janet. "I've thought for weeks that you need a long vacation, and this study cruise, if you can manage it financially, is perfect for you. It's a combination pleasure trip to the Caribbean and an academic brush-up course in nursing techniques conducted by highly qualified people. Not . . . the sort of romantic cruise that we like to dream about." Mrs. Garland rose from the settee. "Offhand, though, I'd say you've had enough romantic complications for one year. You'd be able to relax without feeling that you're not accomplishing anything. Read the brochure and think about it, dear."

Janet mumbled her thanks. Her mind was too numbed to think beyond the phone call she would have to make before returning to the floor. Yet the possibility of going away, as far away as possible, was the only thought that sustained her through the rest of the day.

SIXTEEN

Beth de Haven's body had been shipped to her Long Island home for burial, and three more dismal days had gone by before Janet mentioned the possibility of a long vacation to her aunt.

Denny Reese had become a frequent, if morose, visitor during the time Beth had fought her losing battle with death. Accepted almost as a member of the family, the college student who had loved Beth was slumped in the living room chair when the subject of the study cruise was brought up.

Typically, Cammie made no comment; anything she said might have been interpreted as advice, pro or con.

"I'd sure go somewhere if I could," Denny said. "If I didn't have classes, and if I could afford it."

"Janet can certainly *afford* it," Cammie ventured. (Her glance at Janet added the unspoken thought: "She has plenty of money in the bank now that Dr. Turner's gotten deeper into debt to pay her back.")

"Yeah, well, I'd get away from this gloomy scene if I were you, Janet." Denny swirled a teaspoon through the coffee that had been set before him. "You have these vague guilt feelings

117

you were talking about. I know just what you mean. I've got the same disease, and there's not a blamed thing I can do about it. I envy you, being able to cut out, to try to forget."

"Why should you have any feelings of guilt?" Janet asked. "You might have gotten Beth to settle down, but I doubt it. It wasn't your fault that she wasn't interested in. . . ."

"Forget it." Denny sprang to his feet to retrieve a ball of yarn that had rolled from Cammie's lap. Obviously anxious to steer the conversation away from his abortive "love affair" with Beth, he made a show of admiring the afghan Cammie was knitting. "Hey, that's going to be a groovy . . . whatever it is you're making there."

"Lap robe," Cammie said crisply. "In case Janet decides to take this trip. I'll have it finished by next Monday, if she leaves here then."

"There's still an opening," Janet said. "Mrs. Garland phoned and made a tentative reservation for me."

"Then it's all set, and you don't need any advice from me." Cammie was quiet, her lips moving inaudibly while she made a mental count of stitches, or whatever it was that knitters counted. Then, as if to dismiss her role in the decision, she said, "I hear it gets very cold out at sea. All the movies show people sitting out on deck chairs with doodads like this over their knees."

"On a Caribbean cruise?" Janet smiled.

"Well, it's close to *Christmas*," Cammie told her, as though that explained everything.

Janet got up to pour another cup of black coffee for herself from the carafe. Leaning over the side table, she said, "That's another thing. I'd be leaving you alone for Christmas. We've always had Christmas together."

"I'll lock up the house and go visit Polly MacGruder in Ashtabula," Cammie said. While Janet was trying to identify the name, her aunt explained, "My Fans-of-the-Cincinnati-Reds-Pen-Pal-Club president. Polly's been dying to have me visit her for years. She lives all alone, you know. We'll have a wonderful old time together."

Cammie's enthusiasm sounded forced, but Janet knew better than to argue with her. Besides, another thought had occurred. "You'll be here with just Phyllis until the holidays. I guess . . . I haven't talked to her, but I imagine Phyllis will be going to spend Christmas with her folks in Tennessee. In the meantime. . . ."

"I was going to talk to you about that." Cammie poked her knitting needles into a ball of yarn, setting her project aside. "I don't like to throw any more aggravations at you, Janet. But I've decided that either that girl goes, or I do."

Janet frowned. "You don't really mean that, Cammie!"

"Do I ever say anything I don't mean? I don't want to live in the same house with Phyllis Straley. And please don't ask me for a reason. It's

119

enough to say that I don't care to and I don't intend to."

When Cammie spoke in that adamant fashion, there was nothing to be gained by asking for an explanation. Nor would she have been impressed by the fact that finding new housing for a student at this time of the year presented problems. Furthermore, the housing office at the college would take a dim view of terminating an arrangement because someone's aunt didn't care for a particular boarder. "I wish you'd give me a little more time," Janet said. "Phyllis feels rejected enough as it is. She's told me this is the only *real* home she's ever had. I get a pretty dismal picture of her home life in the past."

Cammie remained seated, her lips pursed, immovable.

"I have had enough memories of telling someone else to get out of this house, Cammie. I wouldn't want a hypersensitive girl like Phyllis on my conscience. Neither would you."

Still no reply.

Janet tried another approach. "I know you feel terrible about Beth. We all do. I know you were very fond of her, and maybe you're thinking that if she hadn't had that fight with Phyllis, Beth would still be here. But Phyllis wasn't to blame, really. You can blame me if you want to. *I'm* the one who ordered Beth to leave. I wish I could undo that. I certainly dread having to do it again, especially to someone who's already convinced that no one likes her." Janet paused. When the invited response failed to materialize, she concluded, "I don't have the stamina for another tearful scene right now. Please give me until after the holidays. When I get back, I'll try to think of some painless way of handling the situation."

"It's your house," Cammie said. "You shouldn't have to ask *me* for any favors."

"Well, you know I'm not going to let *you* leave if I can help it."

The strong assurance seemed to soften Cammie's armor. "All right. I don't want to make things difficult for you. I'll try to tolerate Phyllis, but don't expect miracles. I'm as human as anyone else."

"Maybe I ought to stay here," Janet muttered.

"Oh, don't worry. There won't be any battles. She avoids me and I avoid her." Cammie stuffed the afghan and her knitting paraphernalia into a petit-point bag that was one of her more commendable creations and got up to leave the room. As always, she made an abrupt exit, giving no explanation.

"She's not mad, is she?" Denny asked when he and Janet were alone.

"No, she never feels it's necessary to explain her actions. When she gets ready to leave, she leaves."

"And she says exactly what she means. No yokkydok." Denny sounded admiring. "Tell you something else. Your aunt's a shrewd judge of character. Like, she'll have a phoney already wired while other people are still being introduced."

Was Denny talking about Rick Wexton? Probably not; Janet hadn't mentioned the doctor's exit from her life to Denny or her aunt. Evidently it was just assumed; certainly there had been no questions.

Denny got up, strolling toward the guest closet to get his jacket. "Little tip. Your aunt doesn't interfere in anybody else's business, and she'd quit liking me if *I* did it. Happens that I value the old girl's friendship, so all I'm going to say is . . . if *she* doesn't dig somebody, there's a darn good reason."

"I don't know. I think she's being unreasonable about Phyllis. Look, I'll admit she's no bundle of cheer to have around the house. She's . . . what you college kids call 'on the kissy side.' You know — obsequious. She can get on your nerves. Still, you can't kick someone in the face for being overdevoted to you. It's embarrassing, at times — the way she fawns on me, but from a girl who's desperately in need of friends, you're going to get that kind of . . . superloyalty."

"Yeah." Denny's back was turned as he slipped into the heavy plaid jacket. "Sure."

"Don't you agree?"

Denny looked over his shoulder, a "who-you-kidding?" expression on his boyish face. When he had thanked Janet for the coffee and conversation, Denny made an exit almost as sudden as Cammie's.

He blames Phyllis for what happened, Janet decided. Just like Aunt Cammie, Denny traced the beginning of Beth's end to that petty Sunday afternoon argument that had, ironically, been provoked by Beth. Maybe it was a human reaction to need a whipping boy when people were frustrated by a senseless death, but it was grossly unfair to make Phyllis suffer for something she hadn't done. Janet made up her mind to make up for the cold rejection by Denny and her aunt. If it meant giving up her vacation rather than leaving Phyllis alone in a hostile atmosphere, she would forget the study cruise. If there was one lesson to learn from the mistake she had made with Beth, this was it: You stood by people who needed you, even . . . no, *especially* people who drained your energy and wore on your nerves.

"You're awfully sweet to me," Phyllis said later that evening. "Offering to miss that wonderful vacation just so I wouldn't feel out of place here. I wouldn't dream of letting you make a sacrifice like that for me!"

"I was thinking of the hearing that's coming up on the fourteenth," Janet said. "I know how shy you are. Getting up before a medical board and testifying . . . I know that's going to be an ordeal for you. If you'll feel more comfortable having me around. . . ."

Phyllis' eyes widened. "I'll have to tell exactly what happened, won't I? About Beth's visits to

Dr. Turner's office, and him not letting me put the file away, the way I do when other patients leave. . . ."

"You'll have to tell the truth, the way you remember it," Janet said.

Phyllis nodded, her eyes reflecting her dread of a public appearance before medical authorities. She was ill-at-ease at the dinner table; she would probably die a thousand deaths while being questioned and stared at by the inquiry board.

"If you think you'll need moral support. . . ." Janet began.

"It's going to be awful," Phyllis admitted. "But . . . I've got to learn to stand on my own two feet sometime. I can't expect the one friend I've got to hold my hand for the rest of my life, can I? I've got to start doing some things alone. The way I look. The way I act. I can't expect you to do that for me, Janet."

"That's a good attitude," Janet complimented. "You're beginning to have a little confidence in yourself."

"Oh, I'll be scared to death. Don't think I won't." Phyllis started to twist her knuckles, then became aware of Janet's nervous reaction and stopped. "I won't do that anymore. Okay?"

"Fine."

"Gosh, as much as I'll hate getting up in front of all those doctors . . . maybe saying something that might hurt Dr. Turner, for all I know . . . and you know how I feel about doing anything to hurt *him* . . . I'd hate it even worse if you stayed here just because of me. You need a rest. You deserve it, after all you've gone through." Phyllis hesitated. She was on the verge of tears again, but she gulped them down. "I'd feel awfully guilty if you didn't get to go. And . . . I feel guilty enough now . . . people acting like I did some . . . horrible thing. Oh, Janet . . . why doesn't your aunt like me? I try so hard to. . . ."

"Cammie's an eccentric woman," Janet apologized. "Try to be patient with her, and . . . I'll try to make her understand. . . ."

"All I've done is make trouble for you."

In another few seconds Phyllis would be wailing again. Janet left for the future the confrontation in which she would have to ask Phyllis to leave. Maybe something would happen. Maybe, during her absence, Cammie and Phyllis would resolve their differences. Maybe it was best to let people straighten out their own problems — a despicable man's advice, but not without value!

I'm tired, Janet thought. Tired of these stupid personality clashes, sick of being referee, troubleshooter, confessor, pep-talking coach, and psychiatrist. Suddenly the cruise Mrs. Garland had proposed became more than a vacation. It was a desperately needed escape.

Not until she had confirmed her reservation and started packing did it come to Janet that she had not hesitated so much out of sympathy for Phyllis Straley. *Lloyd.* Though there was nothing she could do to help him — and, in any case,

Lloyd didn't want her help — deep down underneath the thought persisted that she was deserting a friend who needed her. More than a friend. The man she loved. And while it was trying to have other people make demands upon her, it was infinitely more painful not to be wanted or needed by Lloyd Turner at all.

SEVENTEEN

It should have been a thrilling adventure. Except for one vacation she had taken with her father at the age of nine — a brief trip to a Wisconsin fishing resort — Janet had never left Ohio. She had never flown in a plane and had never even dreamed about sailing to exotic tropical islands at a time of year when Danforth lay covered with a mantle of grayish, refrozen slush.

It was all happening now; yet during the flight to New Orleans, from where the study-cruise party was to embark, Janet found herself being tugged back. It was impossible to relax, impossible to concentrate on the colorful itinerary which promised gourmet dinners on hotel terraces overlooking the turquoise sea, white sandy beaches studded with palm trees; and the color and gaiety of steel drum bands and limbo dancers.

Lloyd. Sometime today Lloyd would be facing the medical board. The inquiry might drag on for days, interfering with his work, casting reflections upon his integrity and professional knowledge; for ugly rumors would persist, even when and if he were completely exonerated. And this was only a prelude to what might be a more excruciating trial. If the de Havens instituted a malpractice suit, Lloyd's new and still financially shaky practice would suffer. Worse than that, he would feel alone. Today, with only a panicky file clerk as his witness, he would have to explain the unexplainable: how an unstable minor with a reputation for reckless driving came by prescription drugs that no reputable physician would have placed into her hands.

Going back would serve no purpose. To what could Janet testify? That she knew the doctor was genuinely concerned about Beth? That he had *told* her that Beth had walked out of his office before he could reach a diagnosis? Would a statement like that have any bearing? Hearsay and confidences between two people who were engaged to be married at the time would have no value. Yet wouldn't Lloyd feel less alone if he knew someone believed in him enough to *try?*

Conscience torn, unable to free herself from the feeling that she had deserted Lloyd when he most needed her moral support, Janet completed the flight in a daze. Sights that should have delighted her as the airport limousine purred toward her hotel blurred before her eyes.

He doesn't need me, Janet tried to convince herself. *There's nothing I can do. In a few days it will all be forgotten and I'll feel like a fool, going back home, missing this fabulous opportunity.*

After two days of sightseeing with the other nurses in the party, there would be a get-acquainted party with other passengers on the luxurious cruise ship. In the flurry of making new friends, seeing new sights, enjoying new experiences, the tragedy and its aftermath would be forgotten. Besides, wasn't the object of this vacation to get away, to erase the old miseries, to forget Lloyd Turner?

Janet strode into the plush lobby of the hotel, grimly determined not to look backward. She was going to enjoy herself. This was the beginning of. . . .

Janet had signed the hotel register, explaining that she was with the Professional Tours group, when the young man behind the desk muttered, "Leland . . . Leland. Room 407. I believe there's a wire for you, Miss. Just a moment, please."

Janet held her breath while the clerk turned to examine the wall of keys and mail cubicles behind him. Taking her cue from her aunt, she had always associated telegrams with dire news.

"Yes, here it is, Miss Leland," the clerk said. He casually handed the yellow envelope to Janet.

Janet ripped the envelope open and unfolded the telegram, her hands shaking convulsively. A few seconds later, when she had slipped the message into her handbag, the clerk said, "I'll have the bellhop take your luggage and show you to your room, Miss. You'll find some of your party in the Sky Room, if you'd like to join them."

"Thank you, but I . . . won't be staying," Janet said. "Can you help me get the next flight back to Cincinnati?" For no special reason, she added, "I make connections there for Danforth. That's where I live."

"No bad news, I hope."

"I don't know," Janet told him. "I really don't know."

The clerk was looking at her strangely as he dialed the airline office number, probably wondering what sort of a creature traveled across the country to join a cruise party, only to turn around and go back home again on the basis of a telegram she didn't understand.

Janet could not have explained to him that although the message was unclear, a minor miracle had taken place. The wire had read:

GIVING YOU FIRST AND LAST PIECE
OF ADVICE.
COME BACK IMMEDIATELY. LOVE.
CAMMIE

EIGHTEEN

In spite of her anxiety to get home, Janet spent the night in New Orleans. Preholiday travel was heavy, and the first available flight got her to Cincinnati at eleven the next morning. Waiting for a plane to take her to Danforth would have delayed her there until late afternoon; Janet made the last leg of her return trip by bus.

There was no response when Janet phoned her home from the bus station in Danforth. A call to a surprised Mrs. Garland revealed that the medical board was in session in the hospital's administration office. "Dr. Harrison contacted everyone who knew anything about Beth de Haven's personal habits. I imagine he'll want to talk to you, too. Or were you summoned? Why did you . . . ?"

"I'll tell you later," Janet said. From the public phone outside the bus station she saw a taxi pulling up to the cab stand. Leaving her luggage in the baggage station, propelled by an intuitive sense of urgency, Janet ran to the curb, instructing the waiting cabbie to get her to Danforth Hospital as soon as possible.

The driver, son of a former neighbor, knew Janet by profession, if not by name. "Got an emergency over there?" he asked.

He must have been as bewildered as the room clerk in New Orleans when Janet replied, "I think so. I'm not sure."

"Hope nobody's hurt bad," he said.

"He *might* get hurt," Janet said vaguely. Then, seeing the cabbie's bewildered expression in the rear-view mirror, she added, "He's a wonderful doctor. I hope you can get me there before it's over."

It made no sense, Janet realized. But she was too weary for an explanation. The cab driver shrugged his shoulders slightly. In spite of the icy streets, he reached the hospital in record time; an emergency, however confusing it might be, was still an emergency.

At the door to the paneled room in which hospital board meetings were usually held, Janet identified herself to one of the administration office stenographers who had evidently been posted there to screen out anyone who was not concerned with the case. "Miss de Haven lived at my house," Janet explained.

Motioning for silence with her index finger, the girl opened the door for Janet. Seated at the long walnut conference table were perhaps twelve of the hospital's staff doctors. They barely noticed Janet's entrance. Lloyd Turner was among those who did, though he showed only a fleeting recognition.

Dr. Harrison, the hospital's Chief of Staff, presided at the head of the table, his chair facing the door. Janet caught a glimpse of a woman seated at the other end of the table, her back turned so that Janet could not see her face. Apparently Dr. Harrison had been questioning the woman; at the moment he was asking a stenotypist at his side if she had heard the last statement clearly.

A double line of folding chairs had been set up along the wall. Most of them were occupied. Among the few people present, Janet saw her aunt and Denny Reese. Janet walked soundlessly over the heavily carpeted floor, skirting the table to seat herself next to Cammie.

Cammie's fingers reached out to press Janet's hand. "I'm glad she didn't see you," Cammie whispered. "She might change her tune if she did."

Janet's attention was directed to the conference table. It took several seconds before she realized that the witness, whose face she had not seen until then, was Phyllis Straley. But this was not Phyllis Straley as Janet knew her! Her still drab-colored hair had been frizzed into a coiffure that sat on top of her head like a monstrous bird's nest, accentuating the harsh, bony lines of her face. An unsuccessful attempt had been made to make the thin lips fuller; the cupid's bow Phyllis had outlined with garish purple-pink lipstick added to her too-white makeup to create a ludicrous, clownish effect. Inexpertly applied mascara hardened her chronically red-rimmed eyes. Worst of all, Phyllis had decked herself out in a sleazy royal blue sateen party dress, with a low décolletage that might have been sexy on a buxom barmaid, but only managed to expose Phyllis' stooped shoulders and angular collarbone. Cheap rhinestone jewelry glittered from her ears and wrist. The total effect, besides being outrageously out of place, was pathetic.

Janet barely had time to recover from seeing Phyllis Straley's appearance, when the second shock hit her; Phyllis had apparently been in the middle of her testimony when Janet entered the room. She was going on now, in a fervent, emotion-charged voice that was as incongruous in the sedate meeting room as her attire. But it was not how she was relating her story, but what Phyllis was saying that stunned Janet.

"*I know* Dr. Turner didn't write any prescriptions for Miss de Haven. All he did, both times she came to the office . . . he tried to get her to see a neurologist. And a psychiatrist. I know, because she was mad about it. She drove me home, and all the way she kept saying that he *could* have given her some pills and helped her out, but he refused to do it until she agreed to a full examination. Beth wouldn't do that. All she wanted from Dr. Turner was drugs."

Dr. Harrison winced at the girl's shrill tone. Trying to set a more dignified tone, he asked quietly, "You don't believe the patient consulted Dr. Turner in the hope of getting relief from. . . ."

"She didn't suffer from any headaches!" Phyllis spat out the words vindictively. "If she did, it was because she gulped down pills like

134

candy. Miss Leland asked me to get something from Beth's dresser drawer one day . . . *Janet Leland*, not the one who's here today; the aunt wouldn't know about this. . . ."

Janet and Cammie exchanged knowing glances, astounded by the obvious lie.

"I found enough pills to stock a drug store — hidden away under Beth's sweaters," Phyllis concluded.

"Did you tell Dr. Turner about this?" one of the other doctors asked. "Or the people you were staying with?"

Phyllis appeared confused, but only for an instant. "Oh, I'm sure the Lelands must have known about it. I don't want to make trouble for anybody, but they should have warned Dr. Turner. It just happened that Janet Leland wasn't on very good terms with Dr. Turner at the time. They had been engaged, and Dr. Turner broke it off because she was jealous. . . ."

"We don't want to hear any personal details, Miss Straley." Dr. Harrison scowled his annoyance. "Please confine your. . . ."

"But this has a *lot* to do with the case! If Janet Leland had told Dr. Turner what she knew. . . ."

"I'm still wondering why *you* didn't inform Dr. Turner," a member of the board asked. "You're employed in his office, aren't you, Miss Straley?"

Phyllis colored. "Yessir, but . . . he didn't like to mix . . . well, it was like he didn't let me see the file on Beth de Haven because he's very ethical. Since I knew her personally, he felt she was entitled to privacy, so he didn't let me see her medical record — the way I see the cards of other patients. Dr. Turner is so conscientious, so careful about professional ethics."

The Chief of Staff's irritation was plainly visible now. "No one here questions this, Miss Straley. Could you give us your opinion as to where Miss de Haven secured the drugs that you say she did *not* get from Dr. Turner?"

"I can't name any names." Phyllis intoned the phrase mysteriously, making the most of a dramatic moment. "I know she went out of her way to date interns. Fellows who worked in the lab. Anybody who had access to barbiturates. I guess she dropped anyone who wouldn't give her what she wanted. Or they'd come through once and then they were afraid to supply any more and she wouldn't go out with them again."

"She told you this?" Dr. Harrison persisted. "Or is this your assumption?"

Phyllis stared at the tabletop. "Anybody could have seen it. The Lelands . . . anybody. I'm sorry now that I didn't tell Dr. Turner. I thought it was up to Miss Leland. I didn't know that I was the only one who appreciates what a wonderful person he is — that he wouldn't do anything . . . *anything* wrong, because he's the most honest, sincere, kind person in the whole world. People took advantage of him, and now they won't stand by him. I'm not like that. I'd die before I'd let anyone say he isn't the finest man that. . . ."

Janet sat frozen in her chair, listening to a

volley of praise and declarations of loyalty that could only have come from a neurotic female who was desperately in love with a man. Phyllis' baring of her long-suppressed emotions would have been pitiable, if she had not enmeshed others in her twisted plan to win Lloyd's love. Everything that had once been puzzling was glaringly clear now: Phyllis had played one person against another, created jealousies, invented lies, solicited sympathy and confidence, using everyone who tried to help her for one end only. And this was the culmination of her efforts — this moment when Lloyd would see her as his one loyal, devoted friend, the only woman whom he could trust. This was Phyllis Straley's time of near-triumph, and she had decided to make herself "glamorous" in his eyes, as well.

Janet recalled conversation after conversation with Phyllis, the girl's shallow intrigues revealed under a stark white light, now that she had exposed her motivation. The lies about Lloyd's romantic interest in Beth! The attempts to undermine Janet's confidence in Lloyd, not only as a doctor but as a man! The insistence that Janet take her "well-earned rest." Did she think that Cammie wouldn't report what she had said here today? Or did Phyllis believe that she would accomplish her goal during Janet's absence? It wouldn't matter what anyone thought, once Lloyd had closed his arms around Phyllis in gratitude and love.

A plan like this could only have been born out

of unimaginable frustration. Janet tried to visualize the torment that had produced Phyllis Straley's web of lies, but it was entirely beyond her imagination. Janet shuddered, her stomach churning with a sudden nausea.

As the naked exposure of emotion continued, Lloyd shot an embarrassed, pleading glance at Dr. Harrison. The latter, equally uncomfortable, cut off Phyllis' maudlin tribute by saying, "Thank you, Miss Straley. We appreciate your coming here this afternoon. If we have any more questions. . . ." His voice trailed off, and Phyllis, somewhat reluctantly, got up from her chair. She made an attempt at an exit that was probably meant to be either slinky or dignified. Whatever her intentions, Phyllis turned from the table, wobbled on the uncustomary spike-heeled pumps, and stumbled. She was recovering her balance when she caught sight of Janet. Already white from makeup, her face drained of all its color. For a moment she looked as though she might faint. Then, either because she was too weak to reach the door, or because Phyllis had decided that her triumph was now secure, she lifted her head in a pseudoqueenly gesture and made an ungainly walk toward one of the unoccupied chairs. Apparently she had no intention of leaving. She sat down primly, a comfortable distance away from Janet, Cammie and Denny Reese.

Dr. Harrison frowned. There was no doubt that he had expected the girl to leave, but evidently there was nothing more of a confidential nature to discuss, and he must have decided not to make an issue of the matter. "I think we've covered all the information we need," he said. "Unless someone else has a question?" He looked around at the table. "Dr. Spires? Dr. Turner?"

There was a brief silence, and then it was Denny Reese who was on his feet, his voice shaky as he said, "Doctor Harrison?"

Everyone at the table turned attention to the red-haired college student. Dr. Harrison said, "Is there something you would like to add?"

Denny nodded nervously. "Yessir. I told you yesterday that . . . Beth asked me to get codeine for her and I refused."

"Yes."

"Well, that was true. What I didn't tell you was . . . I didn't want to hurt any other guys . . . pharmacology students or . . . interns. I couldn't tell you who *did* come across, anyway. But . . . what Miss Straley says is right. Beth told me she was getting all the drugs she wanted from somebody who. . . ." Denny's voice choked, then he made a fresh start. "The way she put it was, a guy who cared more about her than I did. The Lelands *didn't* know she was taking drugs. Beth was too clever to let anybody know. When she was high, everybody figured she was . . . happy and enthusiastic. She'd go somewhere and hide when she was down."

Denny took a moment to compose himself,

then he turned a disgusted glance at Phyllis Straley. "Beth was so careful around the Leland house, if anybody saw she had a cache of pills, they had to be snooping through her personal belongings when she and the Lelands were out of the house."

Phyllis made an indignant sound and Dr. Harrison cleared his throat meaningfully.

"I'm sorry," Denny said. "I just wanted everybody to know Beth *was* a sick girl. She put on this happy front, but I know she was miserable because her folks were always fighting and talking about a divorce. They didn't have much use for Beth. And she *did* have terrible headaches. Maybe they were psychosomatic, I don't know. But I wanted to help her because I. . . ."

Denny paused again, fighting to hold back tears. "I loved her very much. Maybe if I had gotten her the drugs she asked for, she wouldn't have dropped me, and maybe I could have reached her. One thing I do know, though . . . one thing Phyllis Straley didn't lie about. Beth stopped seeing Dr. Turner for the same reason she stopped seeing me. She was out to kill herself, one way or another. And she *told* me Dr. Turner . . . the way she put it . . . Dr. Turner wasn't any more of a 'friend' than I was. Beth was only bitter like that when she got desperate for pills *and couldn't get them.*"

Denny shifted from one foot to the other, murmured, "I guess . . . that's all I wanted to say," and sat down. For a few seconds the room was deadly still, after which Dr. Harrison thanked those present, especially Dr. Turner, for their cooperation. There was no reason, Dr. Harrison said, for any further sessions. His tone implied that the matter would not end there, but finding the person or persons who had supplied Beth with barbiturates and codeine was not a part of this inquiry. As far as Lloyd was concerned, the case was closed.

NINETEEN

Janet had lingered behind in the conference room, telling Cammie and Denny about the hectic round trip to New Orleans, thanking her aunt for the telegram, and allowing Phyllis Straley to slip out unnoticed.

"Let her go," Janet whispered as the figure in royal blue sateen eased out into the foyer. "I've had a couple of rough days. I'm not any more anxious to listen to tearful explanations than Phyllis is eager to make them."

Cammie pulled on her gloves. "Pretended that she hadn't seen you," she sniffed. "Well, you won't have to dread a bath of tears at home, dear. I broke my promise to you after Denny told me what happened here yesterday."

"Phyllis wasn't even asked to be here yesterday," Denny explained. "She practically forced her way in, putting on a big show about how Dr. Turner's 'enemies' were trying to ruin him, how he was being 'persecuted', and how she would stand by him no matter what anyone said. Dr. Harrison came close to losing his temper, but he promised she'd get to have her say this afternoon. Only way he could get her out of here without force. Dr. Turner was so embarrassed, all he could do was look daggers at Phyllis. It was so darned obvious she's got this big case on him."

"It's always *been* obvious," Cammie said. "At least it was to me." She lowered her voice. "And to Beth. That was what the argument was about in our kitchen that Sunday. Beth calling Phyllis a vicious little sneak for telling lies . . . breaking up your engagement to Dr. Turner."

"Why didn't you *tell* me these things?" Janet demanded. "Cammie, there's a difference between trying to run somebody's life and. . . ."

"I sent you the wire, didn't I?"

The doctors had moved out of the room. Lloyd had been too absorbed in conversation with Dr. Harrison to greet Janet. She looked out toward the foyer now, wishing that he were alone, wondering if he would listen to an apology — or if it would matter to him when she made it.

"I was ready to get you back here when I saw her nibs leaving the house yesterday, decked out like a beer hall hostess. Whole new outfit," Cammie said. "I knew what she was up to. Not that I thought Dr. Turner was going to be impressed. I just thought, after Denny told me what she'd said, you ought to be around to hear it for yourself. Best way to learn anything. Firsthand."

They moved toward the door, Denny probably sharing Janet's thought: If Cammie had given advice, would Beth have been allowed to leave the house? Wouldn't Janet have asked Phyllis to leave instead?

Denny must have been asking himself the

same questions. Near the door he stopped, turned to Janet and said, "Sometimes we hold back saying things because we don't want to create trouble. Yesterday, when I was asked to testify, I told the board I didn't give drugs to Beth. I was trying to avoid turning the spotlight on some poor lovesick guy who did. It could blow his whole career, I figured. All I accomplished was . . . I didn't do anything to clear Dr. Turner. I had to be shamed into telling the whole truth. By Phyllis, of all people."

"Broke my promise," Cammie said to no one in particular. "I was so furious last night, I really sailed into that weeping willow. Funny thing. I found out she's been so busy mooning about Dr. Turner, she's gotten too far behind in her classes to ever catch up. She didn't *intend* to stay at our place, she said. She's going to quit school and work for the doctor full time."

"Does he know that?" Janet asked.

"She moved out bag and baggage last night," Cammie told her. "And the first thing Dr. Turner knew, he had her on his doorstep. He phoned me this morning wanting to know what was going on. I guess he had a time getting rid of her — finally put her back into a cab and shipped her off to a hotel. She was wearing *red* satin at the time, I'll have you know. With gold sequin trim."

It wasn't necessary for anyone to comment that Phyllis was in need of psychological help. It was even less necessary when the trio stepped out into the hall to find that Phyllis had not made a discreet disappearance. Evidently secure that she had finally accomplished her purpose, she had cornered Lloyd Turner, and anyone within a fifty-foot radius could hear her thin, nasal voice. "You knew you could count on me, didn't you, Dr. Turner? That's what friends are for. When nobody else believes in you, you need somebody who'd do anything for you . . . anything in the world, the way I'd do anything in the world for you. Actually, we're more than friends, because when people go through a terrible thing like this together, they. . . ."

Phyllis stopped short as she saw that she was no longer alone. As she approached, Janet fixed the girl with a stare that could only have been sorrowful; she felt nothing but pity for Phyllis — pity and disappointment. For a moment Phyllis tried to repeat her earlier, lofty pose. Then she made a nervous sound, one half dismissing laughter and the other a more typical whimper.

Janet intended to pass by with her aunt and Denny, resigned to saying nothing, because there was really nothing to say. She was unprepared for the sudden outburst from Phyllis:

"You must have misunderstood. I didn't mean that you knew Beth was taking drugs. You . . . you *did* send me to look into her dresser. Don't you remember? You told me to. . . ."

Phyllis looked around her wildly, seeing only contempt or pity in everyone's eyes. "Maybe you forgot. You've been so busy. You couldn't have known the things Beth did behind your back. . . ."

"Like having clandestine dates with me?" Lloyd's tone was as level as his stare.

"I never said. . . ." Phyllis gasped. "I don't know where you'd get the idea that I. . . ." She faltered, her clown-painted face distorted by panic. "You're all trying to trap me into saying something. I haven't done anything wrong. I made a . . . few mistakes, maybe, but you know how nervous I get in front of people. I may have said . . . whatever you think I said wrong, I did it to help Dr. Turner. Next to you, Janet, he's . . . you know how I feel about you. You're. . . ." The stony silence was too much for Phyllis. "Stop looking at me that way!" she cried. "I can't help it if I'm not beautiful, like you and . . . like that . . . that *drug fiend* your mean old aunt was so crazy about! At least I'm decent! I was brought up in the path of righteousness! I'm *loyal* to Dr. Turner. I'd work for him and slave for him. . . ."

"Miss Straley. . . ."

Lloyd's effort at calming the girl's rising hysteria was wasted. "You're all sinful people! You're cruel to me, just because I'm poor and I try to live a clean, God-fearing life and I don't paint myself up like a hussy and wear shameful. . . ."

Phyllis must have realized, suddenly, the incongruity of her words. She sucked in a wheezing breath, and her big-knuckled fingers fell to touch the gaudy fabric of her dress. A terror of the hellfire and brimstone that had been pounded into her consciousness blazed from her eyes. "You did this to me! I didn't fall from grace until you started teaching me your worldly ways." Phyllis flung herself around in a final, desperate attempt to appeal to Lloyd. "You're a God-fearing man. You don't want to be married to a woman who'll go catting around all night, the way. . . ."

"I think I've heard all I want to hear," Cammie said.

She was already striding toward the hospital's main floor reception room when Phyllis broke down completely. "I hate you!" she shrieked. "I hate all of you! You're evil, wicked people and *I-hate-you-ou-ou!*"

The last wail was accompanied by a dash toward the exit doors at the far end of the lobby. Phyllis was sobbing hysterically as she raced past Cammie.

"She's liable to do something stupid," Denny said. He, too, hurried out of the administration office area, apparently bent on a compassionate mission.

"Denny's right," Janet murmured. "She shouldn't be allowed to run around loose in that condition."

Lloyd released a deep sigh. "Too much!" was all he said.

Janet started to follow her aunt, paused, and then turned back. "There are quite a few nutty females running around loose," she said. "I have an idea Phyllis will be hopping a bus . . . heading back to her own element. At least I'll have access to a good headshrinker here in town."

A faint, weary smile crossed Lloyd's face. "You?"

"Me," Janet said flatly. "I had to be crazy to believe Phyllis' word against yours. I couldn't have been too stable mentally. . . ." Their eyes met, and the rest of Janet's sentence was barely audible. ". . . To let you get away from me, Lloyd."

"That wasn't very bright, was it? They tell me I'm a terrific catch."

"Could you not make fun of me?" Janet said. "It isn't easy to admit I've acted like an imbecile. It's too late, but . . . I did want you to know I'm . . . sorry, Lloyd."

There was interminable silence, and Janet's spirits plunged. It *was* too late. Lloyd had had his fill of emotional crises. He wanted to get back to work, to forget the turmoil that had been imposed upon him because Janet had decided to take strangers into her home.

Tears were threatening Janet's composure when she heard Lloyd say, "I phoned Cammie this morning. Bet her a ceramic kiln against one of her chicken paprika dinners that you wouldn't turn around and come back when she sent you that wire."

"She *told* you she sent . . . ?"

"I guess I'm going to have to set your aunt up as a pot-maker. Maybe I was crazy, too . . . thinking you didn't care enough to come back.

Lost a good dinner, but . . . maybe I've gotten back something I . . . thought I'd lost."

"Come to dinner anyway," Janet said. She looked up at Lloyd, hopeful. "Tonight?"

He nodded. "Better catch up and tell Cammie to fix plenty. It's been a long time, Janet. A long, long time."

TWENTY

Denny Reese had joined them for Cammie's Hungarian-style specialty. Still far from cheerful, he reported that Janet's guess had been accurate; he had helped Phyllis Straley board a bus at five-forty-seven. Paranoiac and tearful, she had announced that she wouldn't be back.

They had all agreed that Phyllis was more pathetic than she was despicable, and shortly after dinner Denny had excused himself. He would be depressed for a long time to come, Janet suspected. But Denny was young, and he had a capacity for burying himself in his studies. His experience with Beth would someday be recalled as a painful part of his education.

Cammie had served their coffee in the living room, and after Denny had said good night and gone, she began to fidget. Looking at her aunt, Janet could see that her brain was trying to produce an urgent reason for going to her room. The best excuse Cammie could produce was, "Your luggage got here from the bus station, Janet. I should really unpack all those clothes for you. You'll be needing. . . ."

"I won't need resort clothes tomorrow morning," Janet assured her. She crossed the room to toss a piece of cordwood into the fireplace. "First place, I'm going to sleep until a week from next Wednesday. And when I get up, I doubt I'll want to put on shorts and a halter."

Cammie glared at her, her eyes asking, "Don't you want to be alone with Lloyd, you nincompoop?"

Lloyd stretched out in his armchair, looking like a long-lost son who has come home. "I've always wanted to see the Caribbean Islands. I hope you don't ever hold it against me, Janet . . . making you miss a trip you'd already paid for."

Cammie had started poking sequin designs into a silk ball Christmas tree ornament. Now she set the bauble down on a lamp table and got to her feet. "I never thought too much of that setup, anyway. Running around with a pack of females, every one of them thinking the boat's going to be crowded with handsome bachelors. And, of course, it wouldn't be. In my opinion, romantic places are intended for honeymoons, not sitting around with a lot of spinster nurses, learning something you already know."

Janet felt herself blushing. How blunt could Cammie get?

Lloyd laughed out loud. "Is *that* advice, Aunt Cammie?"

"I suppose you think that's an amusing remark," Cammie said. She was tromping toward the stairway in the hall. "I wouldn't presume to give *anybody* advice, Dr. Turner. I merely mentioned a perfectly obvious fact."

Lloyd was still laughing as Cammie's footsteps

pounded up the stairs. After a while he said, "You know, I've missed her. Cammie has a way of restoring my perspective."

Janet had returned to the fireplace, poking the new wood deeper into the glowing coals. "She's about as subtle as a bulldozer."

"Honest and direct to the point." Lloyd had walked across the room to where Janet stood. He placed his hands on Janet's shoulders, turning her around so that she faced him. "Here I've been wondering all evening how I'm going to lead up to telling you I still want to marry you, Janet. I never stopped wanting you . . . loving you. And while I'm trying to dream up some . . . devious approach, Cammie hits me right on the head with it. Balmy breezes, long white beaches; the whole bit. The way things are going, I'm even going to be able to afford it."

"Afford what?" Janet asked, knowing, but afraid of being wrong.

For an answer, Lloyd drew her into his arms. His kiss, warm and sweet, held all the promise of a new beginning. When he kissed her the second time, more fervently now, it was as though no new beginning was needed — they had never been apart, they had always been together. They had been separated by nothing more than a bad dream that was already half-forgotten.

They were both breathing hard when Lloyd lifted his lips from Janet's. "Afford a honeymoon on those islands you didn't get to see," he finished. "We were going to be married two weeks from today, remember? Would that still leave you enough time, darling?"

"Time? Two weeks seems like . . . a million years away."

"Cammie said she'll help you with all the arrangements. And you won't have to worry about her being lonely. One sad experience doesn't mean that there aren't dozens of nice, normal student nurses who'd love to move into this house when the February term starts."

"Cammie told you she wants. . . ."

"She needs people to look after. And she's learned a lot. Besides, you're going to be living with me, Janet. Our own home. This is Cammie's place. We'll come to visit, but . . . and she agrees with me . . . a bride should have a home of her own."

They had walked, hand in hand, to the window overlooking the wide porch, and beyond it, the snow-covered front lawn. Across the street, neighbors had already outlined an old frame house with multicolored lights. Christmas was coming, and soon after Christmas there would be spring.

"You've been talking to my aunt," Janet accused. "All this time, behind my back, you've been discussing. . . ."

"We weren't 'discussing'," Lloyd said. His arm fit snugly around Janet's waist. "Keep in mind that I don't have any family except this one, honey." Lloyd chuckled and drew her closer. "I have to have *some* relative to go to when I need advice."

We hope you have enjoyed this Large Print book. Other G.K. Hall & Co. or Chivers Press Large Print books are available at your library or directly from the publishers.

For more information about current and upcoming titles, please call or write, without obligation, to:

G.K. Hall & Co.
P.O. Box 159
Thorndike, Maine 04986 USA
Tel. (800) 223-1244
    (800) 223-6121

OR

Chivers Press Limited
Windsor Bridge Road
Bath BA2 3AX
England
Tel. (0225) 335336

All our Large Print titles are designed for easy reading, and all our books are made to last.